PHILLIP & WHIZZY

TRILOGY

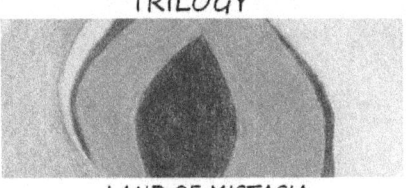

LAND OF MISTASIA

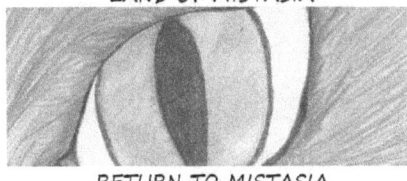

RETURN TO MISTASIA

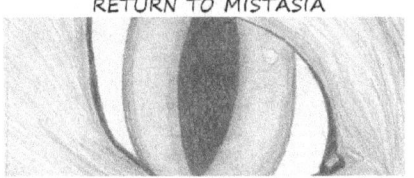

LAST EMERALD

Available

in

Paperback and Kindle™

www.Amazon.com/Kindle

Keyword: Mistasia

LAST EMERALD

PHILLIP & WHIZZY TRILOGY (BOOK 3)

Written & Illustrated by

Christopher M. Purrett

www.LandOfMistasia.com
www.ChristopherMPurrett.com

For my girls...may the end of this adventure lead to the beginning of many more.

Text copyright ©2012 by Christopher M. Purrett
Illustrations by Christopher M. Purrett - copyright ©2012

Phillip Harper and Michael Whizzenmog and all related characters and elements are trademarks by Christopher M. Purrett and Purrett Productions.com

No part of this publication may be reproduced, or stored in a retrieval system, or transmitted in any form or by any means, electronic, mechanical, photocopying, recording, or otherwise without written permission of the author. For information regarding permissions, contact the author through www.purrettproductions.com.

Library of Congress
Purrett, Christopher M.
Phillip & Whizzy: Last Emerald / by Christopher M. Purrett
p. cm.

Summary: Phillip and Whizzy fight to keep King Cragon from gaining possession of the Last Emerald.
ISBN 97809833278-8-2
[1. Fantasy – Fiction. 2. Science Fiction – Fiction. 3. Wizards – Fiction. 4. Heroes – Fiction.]

Released in United States of America
First Edition, February 2012

3

CHAPTERS

LAND OF MISTASIA

KEEGAN CASTLE

DEADLY SPRAY FOREST

MAMMOTH GORGE

ADAIR VILLAGE

CADIEUX CASTLE

MICHI MOUNTAINS

RED RIVER

WOLVERINE FOREST

DRAGON LAKE

CADIEUX VILLAGE

TERASOAR ISLAND

WHIZZENMOG HOME

UNKNOWN LANDS

COLOSSAL LANDS

RACHEL WHIZZENMOG

1

My name is Rachel Whizzenmog, and I have an unbelievable story to tell you. It all began last summer when I was kidnapped by a snake and dragged off to another world called Mistasia. I know that's not what you were probably expecting to hear from a fifteen-year-old girl, but it's true.

Mistasia is a beautiful and dangerous world that I enter through the sliding glass door in my basement. My grandpa once lived in Mistasia long ago as the protector to the King.

In Mistasia, my twin brother, Michael, who we call "Whizzy", and his best friend, Phillip Harper, saved me from the evil King Cragon, who turned out to be a sorcerer.

That's not all...six months later, just before Christmas we all traveled back to Mistasia. When we arrived, it was winter there too and awfully cold...oh, did I mention my brother and I turn into foxes and Phillip becomes a frog in Mistasia?

Phillip, Whizzy and I were brought back to Mistasia by a young vampire bat named, Aevion. The sorcerer, Pierre LaCroiux, was controlling his parents, Goren and Vella. They tricked us and helped King Cragon return to power.

Now, Phillip, Whizzy and I found ourselves trapped, but not in Mistasia...in our hometown of Greenville. We needed to get back and help Queen Merran reclaim her throne from her uncle, the king. It seemed almost hopeless until we realized we had a secret weapon coming over for Christmas holiday, our grandpa...Rainer Whizzenmog.

A LITTLE PRIVACY

2

I looked into the bathroom mirror.

I look awful. I thought to myself.

My eyes were red like I had been crying for days and my hair was a complete mess. Grabbing the nearest hairbrush from the drawer I started to tame my hair. Suddenly, I caught a frightening scent. My clothes were damp and smelled like Whizzy's sweaty gym socks. Yikes!

I need to take a shower before Phillip thinks I'm some wild animal. I told myself. That was probably the best idea I'd had in some time. I needed to relax and unwind. The tension in my neck was causing me to hunch over. I just kept thinking about the poor helpless creatures of Mistasia and the awful things that King Cragon was doing to punish them now that he was back in power. Princess Merran was correct...we needed to get back right away. Every hour we waited here in Greenville, another day passed in Mistasia. Cragon wouldn't wait very long to take his revenge.

The hot water from the shower felt great. It was definitely much better than the cold air in Mistasia. Stepping from the shower, I reached for my towel and quickly wrapped it around me.

I heard a creaking noise while I was drying my hair and quickly stopped. The door was slightly open.

"Whizzy!" I yelled, thinking my stupid brother had opened the door to let in a cool draft. He was always doing dumb things like that to make me mad. I made sure the towel was wrapped around me tightly and stuck my head out into the hallway to yell at him, but there was no one there.

I scoffed. Maybe I just hadn't closed the door tightly enough. This was a very old house and the doors would sometimes creak open. Whizzy used to think it was haunted when we were kids. Pushing against the door harder, I heard it click. Then, I locked it...just to be sure.

When I turned around, I screamed. Standing in the middle of the floor was a small black mouse.

"Aevion! I'm naked," I shouted angrily while pulling my towel close between my legs and crossing my knees.

The small black mouse was the same vampire bat that had taken us to Mistasia the day before. He had been sent back to Greenville with us when his parents, Goren and Vella, the leaders of the vampire bats, betrayed us. Sorcerer LaCroiux kept them under his control, which basically made Phillip, Whizzy and me Aevion's parents now.

"I'm sorry, Rachel. The princess has requested to see you," he spoke while staring at the floor and rubbing his tiny paws together nervously.

"This couldn't wait until I was dressed?" I quickly reached back, unlocked the door and pushed him outside with my hand. He covered his eyes as I slid him across the tile floor and onto the carpeted hallway. "Give me five minutes," I barked and then slammed the door.

I could hear him whimper and then scurry down the hallway towards my bedroom where Princess Merran was hiding.

Standing back in front of the mirror, I wiped away the condensation from the glass. My wet hair clung to my face, and my eyes were still red. There was a knock at the door.

"I said five minutes!" I snapped thinking Aevion had returned.

"Oh, I'm sorry, Rachel," Phillip's muffled voice replied through the door. "But I really need to go to the bathroom."

My heart started to flutter when I heard his voice. It was very strange. Only a year ago I wouldn't have cared if Phillip were here, but now things were different. He made me feel weird and I sort of liked it.

I took a deep breath, "Can't you go downstairs?"

He didn't respond immediately. "Ah...well. I'm not quite comfortable with that, Rachel," He replied. "I had to borrow Whizzy's clothes and they're...well, a little small."

I watched in the mirror as a smile crept across my face. I couldn't help it. I had to see this. Phillip was over six feet tall and Whizzy was shorter than me. Reaching out for the door handle I could feel myself begin to giggle. I stopped to gather myself and then grabbed hold of my towel across my chest and cracked the door open slightly to peer out. Catching a glimpse of Phillip standing there with an orange t-shirt that looked more like a tube top, I burst into laughter. His belly button was staring at me like a creepy eyeball. He also wore Christmas-themed pajama pants with Rudolph and Santa faces all over them. These were also too short and barely covered his knobby knees. He stood with his hands and arms covering his body as if he were naked. It was the strangest and funniest thing I had ever seen. It was kind of cute.

"Oh my gosh, Phillip. What did my brother do to you?" I was laughing pretty hard now and his face began to turn bright red. "Phillip...you look ridiculous."

"Can I go...please?" He begged as he danced on the carpet in his bare feet. "I'd go downstairs, but I can't let everyone see me like this."

"I'll hurry; just wait right there." I rushed back into the bathroom, finished drying off and hurriedly pulled on my night clothes...just an old t-shirt and sweatpants since I had long out grown the little girl night gowns. I didn't even dry my hair, but pulled it back in a ponytail.

Phillip was still hopping around like a frog in the hallway when I opened the door. His dance was quite silly, and it added to how goofy he looked in my brother's clothes. I so wished I had my phone to get video. The door slammed behind me, almost hitting my rear when I heard Phillip yell, "Thanks!"

In my bedroom, Princess Merran waited impatiently for my return. It was just like my mom would have done. Merran, a white cat, was curled up on my pillow with Aevion at the foot of the bed. She gracefully rose when I entered. The banished ex-queen was anxiously awaiting our return to Mistasia.

"Sorry I took so long...I was delayed, Princess," I started to bow then felt silly, so I stopped and then stumbled. It was really awkward which I am definitely glad Phillip didn't see...or my brother. Whizzy would have definitely made some joke about it. "What is it that you wanted to talk to me about?"

"Why does your grandpa wait to take us back to Mistasia, Rachel?" She was very forceful in her tone.

I was shocked to hear her so rude. That was not something she had ever done to me before.

"We need to return immediately!" She continued before I could answer.

"I know, Princess Merran. I want to go back too, but he said he wanted to wait until the morning when my parents are gone," I replied.

The cat tilted her head in a peculiar way. I instantly knew that she didn't understand why that was important.

"I fear that your grandpa has lost his courage, Rachel Whizzenmog."

"No...no, Princess. We can't just leave with my parents here. They will realize that we are missing. With my grandpa here, things are different. When it's just Whizzy and me, we have the freedom to...go play. So our parents expect us to be missing for some time. It is normal. They believe that we are just playing with friends. If my grandpa is missing, that would worry them." I wasn't sure if that even made sense to me so I was pretty sure that Princess Merran would probably be confused.

"It's like the difference between Grace and your servants at Cadieux Castle."

Her ears perked up.

"When Grace isn't at the castle you believe her to be off protecting it. When your servants are gone, you notice that there isn't someone taking care of your needs."

"Ah...I think I understand." She paused for a moment. "Does that mean your grandpa is your parents' servant?"

"No! No, I mean that he is someone that is expected to be around the castle and easily found when needed." I responded.

"Oh...I see."

"Princess, please. You must understand my grandpa will take us to Mistasia. I promise you that. He hasn't lost his courage," I added.

GREEN STONE

3

Later that night, I stood outside the door to the room where my grandpa slept. Whizzy and I had always known him as Grandpa, but he was the original Michael Whizzenmog. His middle name was Rainer. My dad is Michael Whizzenmog, junior, and my brother is the third.

There was a pounding in my chest as I stood, hesitantly, outside the door. I could feel my heart pumping blood through my body like a speeding roller coaster. It was something I had never noticed before our trips to Mistasia. Now everything seemed clearer...more noticeable. My senses were so focused. I wished I could be this focused in math class...maybe I wouldn't have gotten a "C" on my first semester exam.

It was 10:15 pm. Grandpa Whizzenmog was surely asleep, but I needed to know that he was still going. Something in my gut told me something was wrong. I could hear the sound of music from Whizzy's video game in the distance. I scanned the hallway before knocking. No one was around.

My body moved in slow motion. I softly tapped my knuckles on the door as if it was made of glass and afraid it would shatter.

"Why am I so nervous?" I muttered to myself. My hands felt sweaty. "This is ridiculous."

I felt like a criminal. All I wanted to do was talk with my grandpa about a secret magical world where an evil king has taken over and we are trying to overthrow him.

"Oh that's why I'm nervous...I sound crazy!" I answered my own question, which now I realize doesn't make me seem very sane in the first place.

The door opened.

I gasped.

"Rachel?" my grandpa questioned, sounding as surprised as I was to find me standing outside his door this late at night.

"Grandpa," I replied.

"Are you all right?"

I nodded, "Sorry to bother you. I'll go back to bed."

"My dear, come in." He placed his large hand on my shoulder. It seemed so light and delicate for something that resembled a bear claw in size.

He walked me to a single wooden chair at the desk along the wall. Then he sat on the bed. We remained quiet for a moment. I avoided his eyes, but I knew he was looking right at me. Instead I stared at a picture of our family sitting on the nightstand. It was my grandpa's. He had brought it with him on his trip. That is when I noticed this room looked like my grandpa had lived in it for years. The covers on the bed and curtains on the wall were the same, a dark orange like the leaves in fall. Yet, on the nightstand were his reading glasses and chrome-colored watch. His jacket was wrapped around the chair I sat in. I could smell his aftershave on its collar. He had made this room his home. That was when I saw a strange object sitting next to his glasses that I had never seen before. It was small and dark green, yet it glowed like a flame inside lighted it.

"Grandpa, what is that?"

"Ah...that is an emerald. It is a very rare gemstone."

"Did it belong to Grandmother?" I questioned. I couldn't remember her ever talking about it, but she had died nearly five years ago. Maybe I had just forgotten.

My grandpa changed the subject. "Rachel, what brings you to my door at this hour?" He raised his eyebrow.

I still couldn't look in his eyes. This whole situation was making me very uncomfortable. Was I really about to ask my grandpa, a man I loved and admired, if he was a coward? I must be insane to even believe Princess Merran for a second.

The emerald glimmered in the corner of my eye. Suddenly, I couldn't stop thinking about it. It was mesmerizing.

"Rachel!" My grandpa sternly called. "You are acting strangely...like your brother."

I laughed. I was acting very strangely, but lately everything in my life was strange. "Grandpa, why didn't you return to Mistasia?"

"Love," he answered without hesitation. "My priorities changed. I met your grandmother, had a family and moved far away from that life." He didn't appear to have any regrets, but tears formed in his aged eyes.

I didn't know if he was thinking about Grandma or Mistasia.

"Didn't you ever wonder what had happened in Mistasia?" I wanted to know how he left it behind so easily. I had been a wreck since we left and it had only been a few hours!

"I always knew it would find me."

"Find you?" I asked. "Why were you hiding?"

"Mistasia had changed. Everything had changed, my dear." He rubbed the back of his neck.

"How had Mistasia changed? What made you leave?" I needed to know. Mistasia was dangerous now, but only because my grandpa had left it unprotected.

"Sometimes one choice is all it takes to alter the course of everything, Rachel.

Just one." Then he stopped explaining. He seemed very upset.

We sat together silently for a few moments as my grandpa struggled to regain his composure. He rubbed his hand over his mouth and took a deep breath.

Finally, I spoke out, "It is time to return, Grandpa."

He nodded. "Off to bed now. We have quite a journey ahead of us tomorrow."

LEAVING GREENVILLE

4

My alarm began blaring at 7 am that following morning. I am sure that I don't have to explain how early that is when there is no school. Yet, my excitement drove me like it was Christmas morning. I leapt out of bed and dashed to my closet. Quickly changing out of my pajamas, I got dressed, grabbed my wand and went to leave my bedroom when I nearly tripped over Princess Merran. She stood at the door like she was waiting for me to open it. When I did, she gracefully exited. I rolled my eyes at her antics and headed for Whizzy's room.

Grandpa Whizzenmog met me in the hallway outside my brother's room. He, too, was dressed and ready for our trip.

"Do we dare enter?" He said with a smile.

"We had better knock," I replied back with a slight giggle.

He knocked on Whizzy's bedroom door three times. There was no reply.

"Whizzy! Phillip! It is time to go," I called so they would hear me through the door.

My grandpa reached for the door handle.

"Stop!" I blurted out. "Please, don't do that. What if he isn't...decent?"

"Whizzy? My dear he's been indecent since the day he was born." Then he rubbed my back to calm my nerves. "Just wait right here."

Then Grandpa Whizzenmog opened the door, stepped inside, gave me a sly wink and closed the door behind him. Next, his booming voice erupted from the bedroom. "Michael Whizzenmog, wake up!"

I could hear shouting, followed by crashing, and I think someone farted. The commotion continued for a few minutes. Then my grandpa came into the hallway and quickly slammed the door. He was covering his nose and mouth with his shirt. The door handle violently wiggled; then Phillip and Whizzy pounded on the door. They were trying to get out like some hideous creature was attempting to eat them alive.

"What is wrong? What happened?" I screamed in a panic.

"Open this door, Grandpa!" Whizzy yelled in a fit of rage.

"You must pay the penalty for keeping us from our departing time, Michael Whizzenmog." Grandpa chuckled heartily with his nose and mouth still covered within his shirt. His eyes were watering when he looked at me.

I gave him a shocked expression and shook my head.

"It was Whizzy's alarm...do I have to pay the penalty, sir?" Phillip cried.

"Sorry, my boy. Guilt by association." He cackled like a high school freshman.

"What did you do?" I scolded.

"Just gave the boy some of his own medicine."

"Did you fart?" I was most disgusted to imagine my grandpa intentionally passing gas and then trapping my brother and Phillip inside the room to suffer. "Open the door!"

His laughter was growing with every second.

"Now!" I shouted like my mom.

The door flung open causing Phillip and Whizzy to crash to the floor gasping for air. Phillip crawled down the hallway.

"What did you eat?" Phillip squealed in a girlish voice.

"That...was...awful," Whizzy said between deep breaths of fresh air. "I'm gonna get you back, Grandpa."

"Son, you can't beat the master," my grandpa replied, patting Whizzy on top of the head.

"I hope that isn't your power in Mistasia," Whizzy blurted out. "Well, actually that would be pretty cool." He pointed at our giggling elder. "Just don't use it on us...remember, we are on your side."

"You two are embarrassing," I yelled. "Let's just go, please. We have to get to Mistasia and you guys are screwing around."

It was December 16th and my parents had gone to finish their holiday shopping. They would be gone all day. It made today our best opportunity to travel to Mistasia and hopefully return before my parents could realize that we had disappeared.

"We have around ten hours in Greenville," I explained.

"Good that gives us about ten days in Mistasia then," Whizzy replied. "That isn't too bad."

We had gathered in the basement...that was, everyone except Grandpa Whizzenmog.

"Where is your grandpa, Rachel?" Princess Merran questioned.

As we looked around, he finally appeared at the top of the stairs. We watched as he slowly maneuvered the staircase and walked across the basement to the sliding glass door that had served as the portal to Mistasia for our previous trips.

I watched as he adjusted his gloves and then grabbed the handle to the door.

"What are you doing?" I asked.

"I am opening the door," he said with a smart tone.

Whizzy and I shared a confused glance.

"But we have to go through the door," Whizzy said before I could.

"That is the portal to Mistasia, Rainer Whizzenmog," Princess Merran added.

"Well, we can't really go back through the same way you came out can we? Weren't you all banished?" He slid the door open and walked out into the cold winter air.

Phillip was the first to follow. Then we all proceeded to walk out into our wintry backyard.

I carried Princess Merran in my arms, and Aevion sat on Phillip's shoulder. We didn't talk much. Instead we just followed my grandpa as he walked through the backyard and into the forest.

It was cold and slightly windy. It had apparently snowed last night, as a fresh layer of white fluffy snow hung on the tree branches above our heads. A pile of snow slid off one tree and landed directly in front of Phillip.

"That was close," Phillip said, sounding relieved it didn't land on his head. Then more snow tumbled from the same tree and hit Whizzy. Phillip and I laughed at Whizzy as he brushed the snow from his hair.

"That's not funny!" my brother yelled. He looked up into the trees. They swayed in the wind. More snow began to fall toward us. Phillip, Whizzy and I dashed away just in time.

"Where are we going, Whizzy?" Phillip spoke out the side of his mouth. He looked worried. "Your grandpa isn't gonna smoke us out again, is he?"

How disgusting...boys and their bodily functions. How could someone be so proud when they make a room smell so badly that no one can even breathe?

"I know; it was like rotten cabbage and dead animals!" Whizzy laughed.

"Don't say dead animals," Phillip gulped. "We're all gonna be animals when we get back to Mistasia, and I don't wanna be dead!" He cried.

We were silent again. I knew we all were thinking about what Phillip had just said. Everyone looked worried.

"I don't think we can just walk to Mistasia," Whizzy snarled in an attempt to be funny and lighten the mood.

It didn't work.

"No, we cannot, Whizzy. It is just up ahead," Grandpa Whizzenmog responded.

"The river?" I muttered. "But it is frozen over."

"Water makes for a strong magical conductor, Rachel," Grandpa Whizzenmog explained.

"Condu-what?" Whizzy showed how little he paid attention in science class.

"A conductor, Whizzy. It is something that allows another force...in this case magic, to flow properly. Even with the water being frozen, it will let the magic in my wand through...sometimes even magnifying its power," Our grandpa elaborated as he stepped up to the river's edge.

"I'm not really liking this whole jumping into a frozen river idea," Whizzy whined.

"Then you don't have to come," Grandpa Whizzenmog replied. "You can stay home and help your parents wrap gifts." He turned back and smiled at me. I loved it when he picked on Whizzy.

Grandpa Whizzenmog adjusted his snowcap and then pulled a straight wooden stick from his boot. It was his wand. He studied it longingly. It must have been decades since he used it. Running his fingers along the length of his wand, he inhaled deeply.

"Let's see if I remember how to use this," he said.

FLUSHED AWAY

5

I stood impatiently behind my grandpa as he looked out across the frozen river. Drifts of snow swelled on the far side of the river, but there was very little at our feet. Phillip and Whizzy were standing on either side of me as the wind blew at our backs, sweeping the snow across the ice. It slithered along the frozen river top like a snake in the sand. The sun was very low and dim in the sky.

I squinted to see what Grandpa Whizzenmog was doing as he reached into his pocket for something. When he found it, he quickly moved onto the ice.

"What is he waiting for?" Whizzy crassly remarked.

I didn't have any idea. No one did, because none of us responded.

Phillip, Whizzy and I stayed back on shore.

"Do not follow me, kids. I will make sure it is safe first." He stopped only a few feet away from us when a strong gust of wind swirled around and engulfed him in snow.

"Grandpa!" Whizzy yelled then started to run on the ice.

I grabbed him by the arm, "Wait! Don't move!"

The snow blew into the air and Grandpa Whizzenmog reappeared. He had huddled and covered his face.

"I'm fine. Please, stay there," He commanded while wiping snow from his eyes and beard.

The winds had caught us by surprise. Phillip was cuddling Aevion to his chest and I knelt down and huddled around Princess

Merran. Snow was flying around like we were in a winter tornado. It was somewhat difficult to see until my grandpa pulled something from his pocket.

A bright green light made the fluffy white snow seem to disappear. It shot rays of dark green light into the river.

"What is that?" Phillip croaked. He seemed very nervous. I didn't like it when he was nervous...I liked him better when he was confident.

My grandpa raised his arm into the air. He was chanting something, although I couldn't hear him, I could see his lips moving. The light from the object in his hands grew brighter and brighter just before he slammed it onto the frozen river with a loud grunt. A circle of green light rippled out from the object, shaking the ground like a tremor when it passed us by.

"That was wicked!" Whizzy shouted.

Grandpa stood up and backed away with his wand still in his left hand. He eagerly studied the small green object now sticking out from the ice.

"It's the emerald!" I shouted above the rushing winds.

"What?" Phillip asked.

Whizzy and Phillip each listened intently, "A green emerald. I saw it in Grandpa's room last night," I explained as my hair whipped against the increasing winds. "I asked if it belonged to Grandmother, but he didn't say."

Small cracks began to splinter in the ice. They stretched out from the center where the emerald had pierced the ice. The river began to change colors like it was melting rapidly. A large circle formed near where my grandpa now stood.

"Hurry!" Grandpa Whizzenmog shouted as he emphatically waved us toward him.

We dashed onto the icy river and slid to a stop next to the only person who seemed to have any idea what was happening beneath us.

I saw the water bubbling and swirling under our feet. It changed colors directly below us, from a white to clear like the sliding glass door in our basement.

"Hold on!" I heard my grandpa's voice shout, as he firmly grabbed a hold of my arm.

A sinking feeling came over me. Now I knew how Phillip felt almost every single day in school. My stomach flipped and I suddenly felt sick when I watched the icy river-top disintegrate under my boots.

I screamed as I fell into the river, which now swirled like a whirlpool. The water was all around me, yet I wasn't wet or cold. We were in a portal. Grandpa had done it...he had opened the portal to Mistasia.

An orange fish flew past my face. I screamed and then covered my mouth for fear of drowning, but I could breath.

I watched as Whizzy flipped around doing somersaults. He smiled so widely that I almost didn't recognize him. Phillip, however, looked terrified.

Colors began to fade. My brother and Phillip grew smaller until I could no longer see them. Then everything went dark.

Thud!

MY BROTHER AND THE STUPID, FAT DRAGON

6

"Are we in Mistasia?" Whizzy blurted out. It was the first thing I remembered after landing on the frozen ground.

When I opened my eyes, I was no longer human. My skin was covered in golden fur...I was Rachel the Fox, but we appeared to still be in Greenville.

"It didn't work," I sadly stated.

Everything looked identical to the snow-covered river in Greenville...except us. Everyone had returned to their Mistasian forms: Whizzy was a reddish-orange fox, Phillip, a brightly-colored green tree frog with bright red eyes, Aevion a smallish, almost transparent vampire bat, and Princess Merran a blonde-haired, fair-skinned Elven girl.

I searched our landing spot for my grandpa, but couldn't see him. Whizzy and Phillip joined me.

"Are we back?" Whizzy yelled to me.

"We must be! Look at us!" I shouted. I knew that Greenville and Mistasia shared similarities, but the wintry conditions made it very difficult to tell the difference between them now.

There was so much snow piled very high. It had been nearly a month in Mistasian time since we were banished by Cragon Cadieux and the snow had continued to build up.

"Grandpa!" I yelled.

Whizzy placed his hand over my mouth and pulled me down into the snow.

"Be quiet," he mouthed without speaking.

A ferocious roar bellowed out from the forest in the distance behind us.

"Dragons," Phillip said, confirming my fear. "We are definitely back because I didn't see dragons in the trees on the way here." Then he began rubbing snow on his froggy thighs. "Do you have your wands?" He said with a glimmer in his eye.

"Phillip? What are you thinking?" I scolded. His confidence had returned. Water gave him power, so rubbing the snow on his thighs would allow him to absorb the water and strengthen his legs.

That was when I realized Princess Merran and Aevion weren't with us anymore. "Where are they?" I blurted out stopping Phillip in his tracks.

"Out there," Phillip pointed in front of us.

"What?" I replied with confusion. "No, Phillip, not the dragons. Where are Aevion and Princess Merran?" I replied with concern.

"Oh, crap," Whizzy said as he pointed into the open area where we had landed after exiting the portal from Greenville. "They're right there."

Flying in from above, like low cruising airplanes, were two large dragons with Wolverine riders. Aevion began shrieking with fear at the sight of the large scaly beasts.

The dragons roared back in a vocal battle. Any second, I feared that the dragons would blast them with fire and burn them to a crisp. This trip to Mistasia was not starting off very well at all.

"Aevion!" I screamed to draw the dragon's attention without properly thinking the situation through.

"Rachel!" Whizzy barked.

"Here it comes," Phillip yelled in excitement.

The large red dragon swooped down toward us. Its bright yellow eyes glared at me as smoke smoldered from its mouth.

Whizzy and I gripped our wands and pointed them directly at the dragon. Phillip dashed off at a full sprint straight for the angry beast.

"Phillip!" I screamed. I liked his confidence, but this was ridiculous...and now he was in the way! Whizzy and I couldn't use magic without hitting Phillip. "Where is he going?" I asked my brother.

"I think he's going after that dragon," he replied.

Phillip was on a collision course with the flying beast when it spit fire. The heated blast melted the snow at Phillip's feet causing a plume of steam to hang in the air like a fog over a lake.

I screamed, "NO!" The thought of Phillip being melted flashed into my mind.

Phillip shot up out of the steam and landed on the dragon's head.

"Phillip!" I yelled in relief.

He stood on the red beast's snout, between its glowing eyes. The dragon scowled and snorted. Then Phillip ran across its head, jumped over the Wolverine rider, and continued across its back before leaping skyward again. He flipped and landed in the snow just a few dozen feet away from Aevion and Princess Merran.

The second dragon was purple and fat. It appeared to never pass on any meal. Unfortunately, that meant we were on his dinner menu. Its large belly dragged in the snow as it lumbered back and forth keeping Aevion and Princess Merran from escaping. The dragon was taunting them.

Phillip ran across the top of the deep snow to help Aevion and the princess.

The purple dragon's Wolverine rider pulled hard on the reigns, causing the dragon to stand up, exposing its large white underbelly.

Phillip leapt into action, launching himself toward the purple beast. His webbed feet collided with the dragon's belly, only to bounce back like jumping on a trampoline. Phillip was flung into a snowdrift. Crashing violently, he was knocked unconscious.

Whizzy and I ducked behind some snow as the red dragon buzzed by, kicking snow over us like an ocean wave crashing onshore. It trapped my legs and covered most of Whizzy's body. I struggled to free myself, before using my wand to toss the snow aside. Then I freed my brother. We ran to help Aevion and Princess Merran against the purple dragon.

Whizzy shot a freezing spell at the Wolverine rider atop the purple dragon, but missed. I attempted to hit it with an electric shock, but only winged the dragon, causing it to squeal in pain and begin stomping around, flinging snow.

We all scattered. Aevion barely dodged the purple dragon's tail as it slammed down beside him. Princess Merran ran to Phillip, who was still unconscious in the snow. Just before she reached him the red dragon scooped her up in its claws. Whizzy and I attempted to avoid the purple dragon's large feet, which danced around like it was standing in fire instead of cold snow.

A stiff gust of wind pushed Whizzy and me off our feet. As I lay on my back in the snow, I saw the red dragon fly over me with the princess clutched in its grasp.

Quickly, I rolled over and pushed to my feet. I started running after them with my wand pointed at the red dragon's pointy tail.

"Hold still," I said to my target while closing one eye. I aimed and fired a stunning spell at the red dragon just as I was hit in the stomach by the purple dragon's tail.

All the air in my body escaped me. It hurt even more when I landed on my back. I struggled to regain my breath.

"Princess," the word fought to escape my lungs.

Whizzy continued to fight with the fat purple dragon. He had become angry, as Whizzy tends to do. Snow began swirling around him. He slid one leg back and bent his front leg like doing some sort of yoga position. Whizzy swung his right arm back, holding his wand firmly in his paw, and let out a tremendous growl. A blue bolt of lightning erupted from his wand. A thunderclap exploded in the air when the bolt hit the large dragon. It wavered slightly and then crashed to the ground. The vicious beast's horned head landed just a foot from

Aevion, who was shaking with fear. The purple dragon's long sharp fangs jutted out from its closed mouth.

Whizzy punched it in the snout, "Stupid, fat dragon."

I gasped at the sight of the huge beast's head lying in the snow next to Whizzy. My brother was so small compared to it, but he had managed to defeat the purple dragon anyway.

"Rachel?" Whizzy asked with concern.

I replied, as I thought how lucky we were to escape this battle alive, "Whizzy, I'm really beginning to see why Grandpa didn't want to return to Mistasia."

"Grandpa?" Whizzy and I both called out. He was still missing.

CRACKS IN THE ICE

7

I had no idea exactly how long we had been back in Mistasia, but I knew that we were in serious trouble already.

Princess Merran had been captured by a dragon that was no doubt working for King Cragon, Phillip was injured in battle and lay unconscious in the snow, Aevion was so scared that he just shivered, and worst of all...Grandpa Whizzenmog hadn't been seen since we arrived.

What if we can't find our grandpa? I thought. **What would we tell our parents?**

Then Whizzy questioned as if he could read my mind, "What do we do if we don't find, Grandpa?"

"We will find him, Whizzy. Trust me," I stated emphatically trying to convince myself more than my brother. "Just keep looking. He couldn't have just vanished. Think. Just think," I yelled in frustration.

"Where are we?" Whizzy asked.

"You have to be kidding. The giant flying dragons didn't give it away. I'm positive we are in Mistasia, Whizzy." I really didn't want to talk to my brother anymore. I suddenly recalled why I didn't speak to him in middle school.

"Shut it, Rachel. You don't have to be a stupid-head," Whizzy replied.

I couldn't believe what I had heard. "Did you just call me 'stupid-head'? Are you five years old?" I questioned. It was the weakest comeback I had ever heard him use.

"I know we're in Mistasia, Rachel. I am asking you where in Mistasia, genius?" Whizzy barked at me.

"Oh." I looked around again now that the commotion had ended. "I have no idea."

"Aevion, where are we exactly?"
Whizzy asked the frightened vampire bat,
but Aevion only shook his head in reply.

"Well, let's think about this, Whizzy.
There is a forest over there." I pointed
behind the slain purple dragon.

"And they had Wolverine riders,"
Whizzy began and suddenly stopped. He was
intently staring at something. He spun his
wand in his hand like a gunslinger and then
raised his arm and pointed the wand at the
dragon again.

"Whizzy, are you going crazy? That
dragon is dead." My brother was always
weird, but this wasn't the time to be goofing
around.

"But not his rider," Whizzy replied.

Just then a hairy black figure moved
out from behind the large purple dragon's
body. It was the Wolverine. Whizzy had dealt
with them before, the first time we had
traveled to Mistasia. They tried to attack

Whizzy, Phillip and Grace as they moved through the forest to save me.

The nasty monstrous Wolverine glared at us with its evil eyes. Spit dripped from its mouth while its shoulders bobbed up and down with each breath like an apple in water. Then, it charged.

Whizzy fired. The red blast zipped from his wand and slammed into its target. The Wolverine stopped dead in its tracks. Whizzy flicked his wand and tossed the hairy monster. It landed with a sickening crack.

Whizzy smiled victoriously.

Aevion, Whizzy and I ran over to the Wolverine. It lay motionless. I pointed my wand at it.

"These things are really ugly," I gasped.

Whizzy kicked it, "Not so tough are ya?"

"We're on ice," I said aloud.

"What?" Whizzy replied. He still had a smile on his dumb face.

"It's the river! Whizzy, this is Red River," I shouted with excitement. "We always come into Mistasia in what would be our backyard, because we go through the portal in our basement. The backyard would be on the other side. This time we went to the river in Greenville...and so we arrived at the river here in Mistasia."

"So that is Wolverine Forest behind us?" Whizzy questioned.

"Yes! Oh, no. That means the dragon was flying south...to Cadieux Castle," I suddenly felt a sinking feeling. "Whizzy, what if he adds the princess to his statue collection?"

"We'll rescue her, Rachel," my brother promised. "Grace and the princess will be free. Once we find Grandpa...we will save them both," Whizzy replied as he grabbed my arm.

A crack began to form in the ice below our feet.

"Whizzy, watch out," I grabbed my brother and pulled him off the frozen river.

It quickly fractured and collapsed dragging the Wolverine down below. The river swallowed the beast whole.

A strange noise began to gurgle up from the river. Large chunks of ice shot up into the air and crashed down exploding and tossing fragments of ice at us.

A green light began to glow from below the bubbling water's surface. The ground shook and vibrated, making it very hard to stand. Suddenly, a figure burst from the water.

Landing before us was a tall gray-haired fox with black ears and bright blue eyes. He was completely dry despite coming from the river. In his left paw was a green emerald and in his right a straight stick.

"Grandpa?" I asked hopefully.

A sly smile crossed the gray fox's face as he replied, "Yes, my dear."

MAGICAL RIDE

8

I ran and jumped into his arms, giving Grandpa Whizzenmog the biggest hug I could.

"You're alive!" I said while choking back tears of joy.

"Yes, Rachel. I am most certainly alive," Grandpa Whizzenmog replied with a hearty chuckle. "And it appears that you've had quite the encounter." He pointed his wand at the slain purple dragon lying in the white snow.

"Grandpa, Princess Merran has been captured," Whizzy informed him.

The gray fox didn't respond. He stood up straight and looked painfully at the glowing green emerald in his left paw. Then he waved his wand over the stone in a circular motion. It glowed even brighter and then flashed like lightning. When my sight returned to normal, I saw him placing something around his wrist. It looked like a bracelet bearing the same color as the emerald.

"Grandpa," I began when he interrupted me.

"We must make our leave of this place. The castle is still a good distance from here. Princess Merran needs our help." Then the gray fox briskly walked away signaling the end of our conversation.

I watched him walked directly toward our friend, Phillip. Grandpa zapped Phillip awakening him. "We must go, Phillip." Then the gray fox moved on again.

Phillip looked at me with a confused expression. He quickly noticed the fat purple dragon lying in the snow and began to smile.

"Did I do that?" He asked.

"No," I quickly retorted.

Phillip, Whizzy, Aevion and I trekked behind Grandpa Whizzenmog as he walked passed a single tree amidst the deep snow.

"The Friendless Tree," Whizzy whispered to me as he pointed at the lonesome tree that appeared to have run away from the great forest behind us.

I looked it up and down trying to figure out how it ended up by itself. Phillip had his mouth open wide as he gawked at the same tree.

"What is so special about this tree?" I asked. Sometimes I completely forgot that Phillip and Whizzy had this amazing adventure through Mistasia without me. That they experienced fighting dragons in Wolverine Forest, Mermaids on Lake Dragon and so much more when I was held captive by King Cragon's henchmen, Ethan Whizzenmog, in Cadieux Castle.

I was jealous for not getting to experience those same adventures and angry for being held prisoner against my will. Those emotions were long forgotten. Suddenly, they all came flooding back like it was yesterday. Really it had only been six months in our world, but here in Mistasia, it had been more than a dozen years. The difference between our time and that in Mistasia was starting to make it very difficult to keep track.

Whizzy replied to my question about why this tree was so special. "We were here once before. Phillip, Grace and I fought a couple of Wolverines right there," Whizzy said with pride in his voice. Then he looked me dead in the eyes, "It is when I first used my power as a wizard." He beamed from big red ear to big red ear.

"Yeah, Whizzy was awesome!" Phillip responded and then the two gave each other a "high-five" and began to laugh.

I saw Grandpa turn back to watch the commotion. He grinned at me and then came toward us.

"It sounds like you boys have had some amazing adventures here in Mistasia." He patted Whizzy on the shoulder. "We will have plenty of time to tell stories once I have finalized our travel arrangements." He explained while giving me a wily glance.

"Travel arrangements?" Whizzy questioned. "Aren't we walking?"

"Just wait right here, Whizzy, my boy. Your sister and I will be right back."

Grandpa Whizzenmog and I didn't have to go far. We walked only a few feet as Phillip, Whizzy and Aevion stood behind us watching curiously. The crafty gray fox stared at The Friendless Tree.

"What are you thinking?" I asked.

"I'm thinking what would be the best mode of transportation across Lake

Dragon," Grandpa responded with a gleam in his eyes. "This tree will do nicely."

"Really?" I was not fully certain that my grandpa hadn't experienced some sort of brain freeze when he was trapped in the icy river. "'Cuz that looks an awful lot like a tree," I finished my thought aloud.

Grandpa Whizzenmog laughed like I had just told the funniest joke he had ever heard...and I was pretty sure what I had just said wasn't funny at all.

"Rachel, my dear...you are absolutely right. However, you need to open your eyes. This is much more than a tree in Mistasia. The powers that you and your brother possess are a gift almost greater than life itself. When you open your mind to the possibilities, your eyes will show you what may truly be done with those powers." He spoke like a schoolteacher, telling all his most treasured secrets. "Watch and I will show you."

Holding his wand in his right hand, the elderly fox mustered up his strength. He gripped the wand tightly and then slashed at The Friendless Tree's trunk. The wand sliced past the bottom of the tree, yet nothing appeared to happen. Grandpa stood up straight and paused for a moment.

I turned back to my brother giving him a look of bewilderment. He shrugged his shoulders in response. Neither of us understood what was about to happen next. Suddenly, Phillip's red eyes bulged out even further than normal. When I turned back around, Grandpa was pushing the tall tree to the ground. It creaked and snapped before falling and sending the fresh powdery snow into the air.

Phillip, Whizzy, Aevion and I watched in utter amazement as Grandpa Whizzenmog used his magical powers to transform the tree into a wooden ship. The trunk was hollowed out for us to sit in, branches turned into sled rails, and the leaves bonded together to form a large green sail.

"Please, step inside," The tall gray fox proudly proclaimed.

"This is amazing," I announced while climbing aboard.

"Cool," Phillip said as he hopped up.

"You have to teach me how to do that, Grandpa," Whizzy said while Phillip helped him into the ship.

Once Aevion was on board and huddled in the corner Grandpa turned to me and said, "Rachel. This is where you come in. I need you to summon the wind to direct us toward Cadieux Castle."

"Okay." I stood at the edge of the wooden ship and closed my eyes. In my mind I repeated the words "**steady winds**." Slowly, gusts of wind blew through my fur. My ears bent backwards with each passing gust. The winds increased and before long its strength did too. Within just a few minutes I felt the ship beneath me move. The shift startled me, causing me to open my eyes and the winds died.

"What happened?" Whizzy yelled to me from the other end of the ship.

"Don't worry, Rachel. Focus. Just relax and let your mind work," the gray fox instructed.

I again closed my eyes and began to speak the same words in my mind, "**steady winds**." Once again I felt the stiff cold breeze against my furry face and the ship began to slide across the snow. I kept my eyes closed tightly this time for fear of losing focus again. The wind rushed quickly now, forcing the wooden ship to glide faster and faster in the snow.

"That's it, Rachel. You've done it!" Grandpa Whizzenmog proudly called out over the wind.

I could feel the surge of adrenaline moving through my body. It was great. I was controlling the wind, forcing it against the green-leaf sail and pushing us toward Cadieux Castle much quicker than we ever could have traveled on foot.

"Open your eyes, my dear," the calming voice of my grandpa called to me.

I exhaled slowly and peeked out of my left eye. The ship continued to race across the frozen, snow-covered Lake Dragon. A smile burst across my foxy face while I opened my right eye.

"This is awesome!" I squealed in excitement, which must have been really loud, because when I saw Phillip, he was giving me a strange look like I had just grown a second head...it was sort of embarrassing.

The next hour we continued across Lake Dragon and into the realm of Cadieux Castle

The sun had completely disappeared behind the massive dark winter clouds in the usually beautiful Mistasian sky over Cadieux Castle, which was now peeking up in the distance.

Phillip and Whizzy slept while snoring all huddled together. Phillip was spooning Whizzy...I so wished I had brought my phone to get a picture of that. Besides the fact they were animals, I would so be able to use that as blackmail when we got back to school. Aevion was still cowering in the corner of the ship. I sat next to Grandpa Whizzenmog as he steered the wooden ship using a branch from The Friendless Tree that was attached to a large flat stick hanging off the back of the ship. He moved it from left to right, causing the ship to change direction and avoid trees, rocks or large chunks of ice sticking up from the ground.

The emerald bracelet on his wrist wasn't glowing as brightly as it had before. It was almost black now.

"Where did you get that emerald?" I finally mustered up the courage to ask.

Grandpa looked at me for a moment and then quickly focused his eyes on the world in front of the ship.

"It was a gift from King Steven," He solemnly replied, but offered no further explanation.

"Who was he?" I asked, hoping to find out more information about the emerald.

The gray fox suddenly seemed upset, angered by my question. He shook his head and exhaled deeply.

I wasn't sure what to say.

Then the gray fox answered. "He was Princess Merran's father. King Steven

Cadieux was the ruler of Mistasia, and I was his wizard guardian."

"Merran's father?" I responded.

"Yes. What do you know about the princess's parents?" Grandpa questioned me.

"I don't know very much, just that they went on a trip and never returned. That was how Cragon became King," I announced. A light went off in my head, "King Cragon had his own brother killed?"

"He was a part of the plot against King Steven, but he was not the only one," My grandpa began to explain. Then his bright blue eyes grew wide and shock took over his face.

I stood up to see what he was afraid of. "What's wrong?" I yelled over the rushing wind.

"Stop the winds, my dear, or our journey may end quicker than expected," he demanded.

MAGICAL SHIELD

9

My golden-colored furry arms were
stretched out in front of me as I chanted,
"Cease momentum!"

"Focus on the winds, Rachel, not the
ship!" Grandpa Whizzenmog yelled.

My arms fell to my sides. I stared at
my paws, hoping for them to show me
which spell to use. My mind was racing, and
I couldn't think straight, just like at school
when I took my math test. I struggled to
focus my mind...it was spinning around a
million miles an hour. I could feel the lack
air in my chest, like I had forgotten to
breathe.

I heard the elder fox shout, "Rachel,
hurry!"

Phillip and Whizzy had awakened now.

"What's going on?" Whizzy yelled.

"Look at those snow drifts," Phillip said in amazement.

I could see them...huge piles of snow reaching into the sky, like tentacles on an octopus. There was no way the snow should have been piled up like that...it looked like the snow was climbing a wall, but there wasn't anything there.

"What is that?" Phillip croaked.

"What's going on here?" Whizzy squealed again in a high-pitched voice.

"Rachel, now!" Grandpa yelled.

"STOP!" I screamed in frustration. The wind ceased immediately and the previously taut leafy sail drooped down, but the ship was still moving rapidly.

We approached the snowy tentacles too quickly.

Grandpa Whizzenmog pulled hard on his steering branch. He grunted as the paddle cut into the snow.

A white spray made of powdery snow gushed from behind us as the paddle sliced into it.

I dashed to help and grabbed hold of the steering branch with my grandpa.

"Hold on!" The struggling fox growled as the ship turned sideways.

The ship hit a rock, which broke one of the sled rails away, causing us to pitch to the side. Snow cascaded over the side and knocked me down. The steering branch snapped in half. Grandpa stumbled and fell on top of me. Our wooden ship began to widely swing around.

"Cease Momentum!" I shouted in an attempt to stop the ship from crashing into whatever was out there, but it was too late.

Crash!

When I woke up, I was frightened to see Aevion's ghoulish vampire bat face hovering over me.

"Rachel, are you okay?" He whimpered.

"Ahh!" I screamed in his face, causing him to screech back at me and then run away. "Aevion, wait! I'm sorry," I called out to him. A sharp pain shot down my right leg, when I tried to stand up. There was blood in the snow where my furry fox leg stretched out in front of me. A large splinter from our wooden ship was sticking in my thigh. It hurt really badly.

"Rachel!" Phillip's voice rang out. He hopped to my side and hugged me tightly.

I winced in pain.

"You're alive," he happily declared.

"Yes, Phillip. Aevion too," I replied. "Where is Whizzy and Grandpa?" I asked in panic.

Phillip tried to help me up when he saw the splinter in my thigh.

"Rachel, you're hurt," he said while looking me in the eyes. Without hesitation, he lifted me off my feet and into his arms.

"Phillip, don't. What are you doing? Put me down!" I shouted.

"What is going on?" Whizzy barked while lying on his backside.

Phillip walked us over to my brother, who laid sprawled out on his back in the snow staring into the sky.

"Can you ask a different question?" I snarled.

"Not until someone answers my first question!" He snapped back. Whizzy sat up. Snow was stuck in his reddish-orange fur.

"A magical shield, Whizzy," Grandpa Whizzenmog answered in a breathless tone. He struggled to stand and was obviously having trouble breathing. His paw was against his chest.

"Grandpa," I cried while struggling to break free from Phillip's grasp. I managed to get down, but a stabbing pain in my leg knocked me to the ground.

"Rachel, you are injured?" Grandpa asked with remorse.

"Don't worry about me," I replied as I hobbled over to him.

Whizzy ran to help me walk the exhausted gray fox to a large piece of the wooden ship remaining in the snow. He sat down and took a deep breath. I sat beside him.

"I'm sorry, my dear," Grandpa Whizzenmog replied, sounding sad.

"I'll be fine."

"Let me help you," he said and removed the emerald bracelet from his wrist and wrapped it around my thigh. Grandpa grabbed the splinter sticking out of my fur and said, "This will only hurt for a moment."

Grandpa yanked the wooden splinter from my thigh.

I screamed in pain, but quickly covered my mouth with my paws. Tears streamed from my eyes. It was the worst pain I could remember in my entire life. It made getting a shot at the doctor's, feel more like a pinch.

Phillip, Whizzy and I watched as the emerald bracelet began to glow again. It suddenly was alive with bright lights inside, swirling and dancing around. My leg began to glow as well. A warm sensation entered my entire leg, like when it falls asleep and I get that prickliness. I started to laugh...it felt really weird. When it was over, my leg was healed.

Grandpa smiled at us. He took the emerald bracelet back and wrapped it around his wrist once again. The color faded back to black.

"That emerald is wicked," Whizzy replied.

He isn't the most intelligent 15-year-old boy in the world...but he is the only brother I have.

I couldn't stop staring at the spot where the splinter had been. I rubbed my paw across it. It was as if the wound never existed.

"How was that possible?" I blurted out.

Everyone stopped and turned to gawk at me.

"Some things cannot be explained, my dear," Grandpa responded. "This emerald...this last emerald of Mistasia is a very powerful gem. It can perform miraculous feats...or destructive acts, if it falls into the wrong hands."

"Then let's make sure King Cragon doesn't know about it," Phillip replied.

I saw Grandpa glance at Phillip, but say nothing. He moved away from us and reached out like he was feeling for something in the air.

I hobbled next to him. My leg may have healed, but it was extremely sore.

"King Cragon already knows about the emerald doesn't he," I whispered to the tall gray fox.

He stopped his hands for a second...then continued without answering.

"I take that as a 'yes'," I replied now, realizing that we had another problem. We were trying to get into Cadieux Castle to save our friends, yet bringing the one thing that the evil king wanted most...the last emerald. With it, he would be even more powerful.

"What is going on?" Whizzy asked for the fourth time.

"I'm gonna punch you in the nose," I growled.

"Well that isn't very lady-like," Whizzy responded in a silly voice.

I balled my paw in a fist and reached back to slug him, when Grandpa spoke.

"This is a very powerful dark magic," he muttered.

"Excuse me," I asked with my fist still ready to fly.

I saw Whizzy take two steps backward from the corner of my eye.

Grandpa closed his eyes and placed his paw against an invisible object. He began to mumble under his breath. I couldn't understand what he said. It sounded like he was speaking in another language.

His paws started to glow. The light stretched out into the air. As it moved outward, shapes began to appear. Before our eyes, a wall emerged. It was made from a series of tangled vines and branches that covered the entire castle and some of the surrounding village, like a protective bubble.

"Well...now I know what happened," Whizzy said and immediately looked at me. "So I'm done. Promise." He said with his hands up, like he surrendered.

I growled at him and put my fist down.

"How do we get inside?" Phillip asked. "Can we use the emerald?" He added.

"No. I am afraid not. The emerald does have extraordinary powers, but it also has its limitations. The gemstone stores energy from everything around it. It absorbs from this world...but once it has been used, it will take some time to restore the emerald's power," Grandpa said while examining the wall in front of him.

"So what do we do?" Whizzy said finally, asking a different question.

"It's about time," I teased him.

"Find a weakness," Grandpa responded.

SAVING GRACE

10

It grew very dark outside as angry clouds now hung over Cadieux Castle. A few lit windows in the distance peeked through the void, like eyes watching our every movement.

I felt the hair on my neck stand on end as I thought about King Cragon plotting against us as he looked through those same windows. He would most definitely do his worst.

Grandpa studied the magical shield that kept us from entering Cadieux Village. If he was frustrated, I couldn't tell...he seemed so calm. I would have been a mess, and my brother would be throwing a temper-tantrum by now.

"Is there anything I can do?" I offered my assistance to our leader.

"I'm open to any and all suggestions, my dear," He somberly responded.

"Couldn't we try cutting it open?" I asked, trying not to sound too obvious.

"Watch," Grandpa slashed at the tangled mess with his wand the same way he did when he cut down The Friendless Tree only a few hours earlier. Nothing happened. "It is dark magic and very strong."

"Any other suggestions, Sis," Whizzy teased.

"Well, what is your idea, brainiac?" I challenged.

"Dig underneath," He smartly replied.

"That won't work!" I shouted. "Will it?" I whispered to Grandpa so Whizzy wouldn't hear.

The gray fox shrugged his shoulders.

Whizzy used his magic to dig a hole under the magic shield, but with each inch of snow he removed the shield stretched to cover it back up.

"See," I scoffed. "Told you it wouldn't work."

"What about fire?" Phillip added.

Whizzy, Grandpa and I glanced at each other. No one seemed to know what would happen.

Grandpa Whizzenmog asked us to stand back. He shot a large fireball directly at the magic shield. It quickly caught fire. The vines and branches were burning. With each passing second, the wall shriveled up and crashed to the snow. Grandpa blew out the flames with a blast of cold air. Left behind was a hole torched in the sorcerer's magical shield.

"Phillip, you were correct," The elder gray fox spoke in amazement. "And you're not even a wizard. How about that?"

Phillip smiled.

We all entered Cadieux Village through the small hole. Running through the snowy village, we dashed to the edge of the castle grounds.

As we approached, I began to have a bad feeling. It had been so easy to get to the castle. Other than the dragons at Red River, we hadn't had to fight anyone. I quickly looked for Phillip. One of his abilities here in Mistasia is clairvoyance, or visions that appeared to him when he was dreaming...but he hadn't slept since we arrived.

Phillip and I ran to the edge of the field leading to the castle. There, we stopped and stood side by side. Whizzy was on the other side of Phillip, and Grandpa was beside me. Aevion was hiding behind Phillip.

"I have a very bad feeling we are walking into a trap," Phillip said to me.

"You, too?" I replied.

He reached out and grabbed my paw. I felt a tingle in my arm. Then my hand felt damp. I pulled my paw away.

"Sorry, sometimes I forget I'm an amphibian," Phillip apologized.

"It's okay," I replied. I felt warmth in my cheeks. Hopefully, Phillip couldn't tell; I was probably blushing.

"Hey, love birds...we've got company," Whizzy pointed at the sky above the castle.

"I don't see anything," I said.

"Neither can I," My brother replied with his eyes closed. "But I can hear their wings."

I closed my eyes. My fox ears quickly picked up a flapping sound in the distance. "Vampire bats."

"I hear them too, Whizzy." Grandpa chimed in.

In the distance, a light began bobbing in the darkness. It moved briskly toward us and then stopped. The light grew brighter by the second until we could see the image of a man standing in the snow between the castle and us.

"LaCroiux," Grandpa said empathically.

"Rainer Whizzenmog," Sorcerer Pierre LaCroiux sneered. "After all these years you have finally returned. Unfortunately, it is far too late."

"We will see," Grandpa responded.

"No, Rainer...I will show you."

The grounds lit up as if the sun had exploded from behind the gloomy storm clouds, yet the dark gray sky still remained. That made it even more frightening.

Sorcerer LaCroiux stood alone in the snow, but in the distance was a more menacing force. Three great trolls stood along the castle walls, Vella and Goren circled the skies above with nearly a dozen more vampire bats, and slowly marching to the sorcerer's side were nearly two-dozen wolverines.

"Oh, crap," Whizzy blurted out.

"I think I already did," Phillip whined.

"Welcome back to Mistasia," Sorcerer LaCroiux blasted. "King Cragon sends his regards." The smug white-bearded villain replied. "ATTACK!"

The Wolverine Army roared toward us, while the vampire bats swooped in from above.

"We need to split up," Grandpa calmly spoke. "Rachel and Whizzy you must find your friend, Grace. Phillip will come with me. Aevion...hide," He demanded.

I watched as the gray fox and green frog ran toward the Wolverine Army.

"This is insane," Whizzy barked as he grabbed my hand and ran away.

"No stop, Whizzy! We can't leave Phillip and Grandpa behind," I cried as my brother dragged me through the snow.

"We have to find Grace!" he yelled at
me.

"She's that way," I pointed at the
castle.

"We can get into the castle from her
house, remember!" Whizzy said, referring to
the underground passage we had used in the
past.

Goren and Vella crashed down beside
us and screeched. I flicked my wand at Vella
hitting her with a stunning charm. She was
tossed backwards. Goren became very angry
and swatted at me. Whizzy punched him
with a spell, spinning the vampire bat
around before he fell into the snow, ugly
face first.

My brother and I ran as fast as we
could to Grace Tallon's quaint home in
Cadieux Village, but before we could reach
it, two more vampire bats snatched us off
the ground and circled back to the castle. As
we flew by, I saw Phillip jumping around

like crazy. He bounced up and down landing on one wolverine and then crashing into another. Each angry hairy beast fell to the ground in pain. Grandpa cut a path to the castle by blasting his foes with different spells. A fury of various colors exploded from his wand. It resembled a firework show.

A pit grew in my stomach as we approached the castle. We couldn't let these vampire bats take us there. Nothing good could possibly come of arriving at Cadieux Castle before our grandpa.

I still gripped my wand in my paw. To my left I could see Whizzy. I began to wiggle. Suddenly, the vampire bat's grip on me loosened, and I began to fall. I turned to face the sky and shot at each vampire bat, hitting one in the face. The second shot slammed into the wing of Whizzy's captor. The vampire bat squealed and dropped my brother.

We landed only a few feet from each other. My leg was throbbing now where the wooden splinter had been. I could barely stand up, and then my brother grabbed me and pulled me up out of the snow.

"We gotta go," he screamed.

A massive tree trunk crashed into the snow where I had just been. As I followed the length of the big wooden object, I found a hideously large troll at the other end. It had a small head with beady eyes and ears that stuck out like targets on either side. His face was covered in warts and thick hairs just stuck out in random places. He even had one on the tip of his nose.

"Kids," Grandpa called as we had somehow met up with him and Phillip in the middle of this battle. "Are you all right?" He questioned while fighting two wolverines and a vampire bat at the same time.

"No," I began when Whizzy interrupted.

"There!" He shouted.

I looked at the spot where he was pointing atop a tower on Cadieux Castle. There, Grace Tallon stood frozen in motion as a stone statue.

"We need her," Grandpa urged us to complete our task. "You must save her!"

Whizzy and I dashed off immediately leaving Phillip and Grandpa Whizzenmog to battle King Cragon's Army.

FLIGHT OF THE FOX

11

I followed directly behind my brother as he whisked through the battlefield. He blazed a trail in front of us with his wand.

I struggled to keep pace as my leg felt like someone was stabbing me every time I placed my right paw down. It would send a shockwave up my thigh, through my back and into my brain. I thought the emerald had healed me...it only masked the injury. Maybe that was what my grandpa was trying to do.

Some type of sorcery from Pierre LaCroiux still brightly lighted the field surrounding Cadieux Castle. I saw a shadowy figure peering from one of the lit windows of the castle...it must be King Cragon. He is too cowardly to actually fight his own battles, yet he found the time to watch them from a safe distance.

It was so loud. The roar of wolverines, the screeching of vampire bats, then an explosion of magic slammed into my highly tuned fox ears. It sounded like a cross between the Fourth of July celebration and the Greenville Zoo.

Whizzy and I had almost reached the castle when we ran into a very large problem...literally.

The smelly foot of another grotesque troll crashed down in front of Whizzy just as he reached for the handle on the castle's front door. Whizzy's face planted into the anklebone of the troll, and pin-balled to the ground. I slid to a stop, only inches away.

A large droplet of goober splashed into the snow at my feet. I gulped and then looked up to see the absolutely stomach-turning face of our latest enemy.

"AHHHHH!" I screamed like a little girl.

"ARRRGGGG!" the troll screamed back.

I think I actually frightened him too. Unfortunately, this troll must have had a winter cold, because greenish-yellow snot oozed from his nostrils. The troll reached out to grab me with its chunky dirty fingers.

I stumbled backwards and fell. I was trapped.

"Whizzy!" I screamed.

My brother cast a spell to control the troll's wooden club. Whizzy swatted the troll in its thick melon-head repeatedly, while shouting, "Leave my sister alone. You ugly...smelly...snot-nosed...turd!"

After somewhere around 15 swats in the head, the troll finally stumbled. Its eyes rolled back in its head and then it fell backwards into the castle door, smashing it open.

I had taken one step toward the open door when I felt two sharp claws grab my waist and yank me off the ground. It was Vella. She had found us and couldn't be happy with me for zapping her with a spell earlier. Whizzy was gone. I couldn't see him as Vella sped skyward into the dark gray clouds.

I could instantly feel the chill of the air increase around me. Frost formed on my whiskers and snout. Once we reached the storm clouds, Vella stopped. I thought I was dead. The sudden thought of her dropping me from this height sickened me.

"Rachel Whizzenmog," Vella's voice sounded different. "Do you know where my son is?" She questioned sadly.

"Yes." I could see in her eyes that Vella was somehow different...frightened. "He has been with us the whole time."

"Is he here now?"

"Yes. He is hiding until the battle is over." I suddenly realized that when I hit her with a spell earlier I must have broken the hold that Sorcerer LaCroiux had over her.

"Will you take me to him?" Vella asked humbly.

"Of course, Vella, but I need your help first." This was my chance. She could fly me to the tower where Grace Tallon was kept.

Vella gave her consent, and I told her my plan. Together we flew through the clouds and burst out directly above the castle. I pointed to where Grace was being held and she took me there.

We landed safely atop the tower. There Grace Tallon stood, eerily frozen in stone. I wasted little time, and began firing spells to free her. Nothing worked...I couldn't break the magical secret that turned her into stone.

"I can't free her," I said, disappointed in myself.

A rustling of footsteps sounded just on the other side of the door leading out to where we stood atop the tower.

"Hide," I shouted to Vella who jumped into the sky leaving me alone. I searched for a place to hide, but it was a wide-open tower with nothing to hide behind.

The door handle jiggled, but the door was locked. I sighed in relief, just before it exploded. Splinters and chunks of wood flew toward me.

"Protectum," I whispered trying not to draw attention to myself. An invisible shield formed, blocking me from the wooden pieces.

A small figure entered the tower. It was Whizzy. I had never been so excited to see my brother in my whole life.

"Whizzy!" I shouted.

"Rachel!" He hugged me.

"You're hugging me," I said in amazement.

"Yeah, sorry. Got carried away," He replied, quickly letting me go.

"Whizzy, I tried to free Grace, but nothing I tried worked."

My brother just ignored me and began blasting Grace's statuesque figure with an array of magical charms and spells.

After a few moments of frustration, Whizzy threw his wand onto the stone ground.

"As I was saying, I tried to free her before you got here and nothing worked. What are we gonna do, Whizzy?" I was out of ideas.

My brother had developed a crush on Grace. She was very special to him. He stood as close as he could, resting his forehead against hers.

"I watched him do this to her, Rachel. I couldn't help her. It was like I was that helpless little kid back in Greenville," Whizzy tried to hold back his emotions. He placed his paw on her cheek. "Look at how scared she is."

"Whizzy," I wanted to tell him it would be okay. I wanted to tell him that Grace would be fine. I also wanted to tell him that we were running out of time...but I couldn't say anything.

"I'm sorry," Whizzy softly spoke. Then, my brother moved in and placed his lips on Grace's cheek giving her statue a kiss.

My eyes nearly popped out of my head. "Whizzy," I muttered to myself in shock. The only thing I had ever seen my brother kiss was his pillow. I could feel the cold winter air rushing into my mouth as it flopped wide open.

Whizzy stepped back. Grace Tallon's face began to shimmer. A glow moved down her body until it completely covered her. The shimmering light grew brighter and more intense, but I couldn't stop staring. The stone seemed to melt away. All of a sudden, standing before us was Grace Tallon, the Elven warrior, protector of Princess Merran Cadieux, and our friend...and she was free!

Grace began to fall to the ground. Whizzy caught her.

"Grace," he called to her in a panic.

She smiled at him, "Whizzy, you came back for me," she replied in a weak voice.

"Yes," he replied with a sniffle. "I'm so sorry, Grace."

The Elven warrior lifted her head and looked to the edge of the castle tower. "What is that noise?"

DISAPPEARING ACT

12

Grace looked awful. Her usually pretty white hair was dirty and grimy. Her cheeks were dry and cracked and eyes bloodshot.

"Can you stand up?" I asked her, wondering if she would have enough strength to escape with us.

Struggling to her feet, the willful Elven warrior now stood beside her rescuer, Whizzy.

"Thank you, Whizzy," Grace spoke in a humble tone. Then she walked to the edge of the castle tower to witness the battle below.

Phillip and Grandpa Whizzenmog continued to fight off King Cragon's Wolverine Army. The vampire bats had disappeared and the trolls had been defeated.

"We must aid them," Grace commanded.

I knew it wouldn't be long before she returned to normal. It was just her nature to be a leader...and so she led us down the staircase, through the castle halls and out through the broken front door where the troll Whizzy had knocked out still lay unconscious. The commotion in the field around the castle was exciting and frightening at the same time.

We sprinted across the open field to help Phillip and Grandpa Whizzenmog ward off the ferocious wolverines.

"Phillip, behind you!" I yelled to warn him as a wolverine snuck up to grab him. He turned around and dodged the wolverine's attack.

I fired a spell directly into the hairy beast's chest causing it to fall to the snow.

"Thanks, Rachel," Phillip replied with a smile. "Grace!" He called out with joy.

"Great job, kids!" Grandpa Whizzenmog praised. He punched one wolverine in the face and then zapped another. "We need to retreat to the village!" He ordered. "I will afford you some time. Now, go!"

"What about Princess Merran?" Phillip reminded us that she too had been captured.

"We must regroup in order to save her," Grandpa gritted his teeth as he grappled with another beast. "Go!"

I grabbed Phillip by his webbed hand and began to run away from the castle. Whizzy and Grace followed. Grace Tallon quickly overtook us as she flashed passed.

Grandpa continued to keep our enemies at a distance. A green light crept from the tip of his wand, like a whip. He would fling it at any wolverine that approached, cracking the whip loudly.

We nearly reached the edge of the field when we realized the magical shield was still there. Whizzy pointed to where the opening had been burned earlier for us to enter and we ran toward it.

A loud crack of thunder rumbled behind us, causing all of us to stop immediately. Sorcerer LaCroiux had returned. He twisted his braided white beard with his left fingers.

The heinous Sorcerer LaCroiux and Grandpa Whizzenmog locked eyes. Neither spoke a word. LaCroiux just sneered.

"Grandpa, no!" I shouted. It was too late.

The evil sorcerer and wizard fox were locked in battle.

I found myself stuck in the snow completely unable to move as I watched our grandpa brawl with LaCroiux. My legs just didn't work. They felt like heavy cement pillars dug deep into the ground.

"You never should have returned," Sorcerer LaCroiux challenged while waving his hands over the snow stirring it into a blizzard. He disappeared behind the whitewash.

Grandpa split the snowy wall by using his wand as a sword. The slick gray fox maneuvered through the gap sliding on his left side and shot a spell directly at his foe.

LaCroiux deflected the wizard's attempt. "Rainer, you must be rusty. I expected better than that," he mocked before lashing out and knocking Grandpa Whizzenmog down with a wave of snow.

The gray fox jumped back to his feet and dodged two move waves of snow by somersaulting backwards. He retaliated, zapping LaCroiux with a paralyzing spell.

The elderly sorcerer fell to his knees and shouted in disgust, "You are weak."

Then he raised his arms slowly and all the snow around him ascended. "I will show you strength!" He boasted and then flung his arms at his target, pushing all the snow at him. It was too much for the nimble fox to avoid. Grandpa was overtaken by the avalanche and covered in thick, cold snow.

I gasped as my grandpa disappeared from view.

"No!" Whizzy barked from behind me.

It was as though my legs had been released from the heavy weight I felt before and now I was running to help my grandpa. Whizzy followed behind me. I thought I heard Grace call to us, but I didn't care...I was going to help him. Phillip joined us. Grace must have decided to as well because soon she ran up beside me. The four of us approached when Sorcerer LaCroiux swept in front of us riding a wave of snow.

"Going somewhere?" He bellowed.

"Get out of the way!" Whizzy yelled while pointing his crooked wand at LaCroiux.

The sorcerer immediately responded by knocking my brother down with a blast of wind.

I kept moving toward Grandpa.

Grace pulled an arrow from her backpack and swiftly fired, but the evil sorcerer deflected it with ease and fought back, sweeping her aside with the wave of his hand.

"Phillip!" I called out. "Give me time!"

"I'm on it," he replied.

But before Phillip could even attempt to battle Sorcerer LaCroiux, I felt a strange sensation against my fur. The world seemed to be slowing down. Sounds stretched in my ears. It was like I fell down a tunnel. Snowflakes hung motionless in the air before me.

Then a wall of orange light began to move across the field. I watched it engulf Whizzy. When it passed by, my brother was gone. Then it swallowed Phillip and Grace. Next, the orange light attacked me. I was only a few feet away from where Grandpa Whizzenmog was buried alive in the snow when the orange light blinded me.

Then, everything went completely black!

WORKING FOR THE WICKED MONSTER

13

"Grandpa!" I screamed when I felt my body hit the ground. Immediately, something was very different about Mistasia. It was unexpectedly warm. The chill removed from my fur-covered body and was replaced with dampness, like when I just leave the shower. My chest was sore from my heart racing so quickly. I placed my paw against it and opened my eyes.

"No. No, no, NO!" Panic began to set in. This wasn't Mistasia. At least not the one we knew. **What happened? Where did LaCroiux send us?**

I picked myself up and found I was standing in thick blades of dark green grass that reached over my head. They had to be nearly eight feet tall. There was no snow, only dirt in my paws.

Noises echoed all around me, as it grew harder to breath, but not from the lack of oxygen, just fear.

Where are we? I thought.

"Rachel," Phillip's voice sounded off in my head.

I spun around to find him, but could see nothing but green grass, standing like trees, surrounding me.

"Phillip!" I called out, but it was no use. The blades of grass blocked my voice from escaping.

"Rachel, where are you?" Phillip asked me again using his ability of telepathy. He and Grace shared that power here in Mistasia. That meant that wherever we were was at least still Mistasia.

I tried to calm myself down. There was so much noise in my head between

Phillip and my own heart pounding. I took a slow deep breath and closed my eyes.

Phillip, I am here! I thought, hoping to be able to speak to him. He could hear my thoughts, so I would be able to contact him.

"Rachel," Phillip said aloud as he grabbed my arm.

"Ahhh!" I screamed and then punched him in the face just below his big red eye.

The tall frog stumbled and fell backward, toppling over some blades of grass. Behind him was a path in the dense jungle that he had used to find me.

"Phillip, I'm so sorry." I leaned in and gave him a kiss on the cheek where I had socked him. It was really red...I couldn't tell if it was because I punched him or he was embarrassed to be hit by a girl. After helping him back to his webbed feet, we rejoined Grace and Whizzy.

"Where are we, Grace?" Whizzy demanded to know.

She mumbled sometime in elfish that sounded a lot like swearing, and then checked her backpack for weapons.

"Grace, where are we?" I asked, hoping she would give me some information, if she wouldn't answer my brother.

Again she continued to ignore us and shuffled through her collection of arrows. Finally, she blurted out, "Twenty-two."

"Great, now that you have counted your arrows, can you tell us where we are in Mistasia?" Whizzy barked.

"We have been banished to The Colossal Lands," Grace looked shaken and afraid.

"Okay, I get that. Really big grass. Big...colossal," Whizzy reasoned while waving his arms in the air. "Why are all the names here so cheesy?" He turned to Phillip and me for answers.

His best friend shrugged his shoulders.

I did what I have done for most of my life, ignored the fact he said anything at all and moved on.

"Grace, how do we get back to Cadieux Castle?" I asked while placing my paw on her shoulder.

She shrugged it off and stood up. "That is impossible, Rachel the Fox. We are a great distance from Cadieux Castle. It would take a great deal of time to travel back." Grace aggressively shoved her arrows back into her pack.

"Why is there no snow?" Phillip added.

I shot Phillip a dirty look for asking such a stupid question.

"This land does not experience winter like we do. It is perpetually warm in the Colossal Lands." Grace replied as she slung her pack onto her back.

Phillip, Whizzy and I gave each other a nervous look. We had never seen Grace so distraught before. She had fought wolverines, vampire bats, trolls and even sorcerers so bravely, but now she was as frightened as Phillip on the first day of school.

The Elven warrior readied her bow and arrow, "Now we must find a way to stay alive."

Grace had my brother and I dig a trench using magic. Meanwhile, Grace and Phillip built weapons to protect us at each end of the trench. She said it would allow us to survive the night. That sounded like a great idea to me.

I walked past Phillip as he assembled a crude looking weapon. "What are you making?" I asked.

"Grace showed me how to build a slingshot out of blades of grass and roots from the ground. She is gathering pebbles and stuff for us to use to defend ourselves."

"From what exactly? Because she hasn't really explained of what we should be so afraid." I was starting to become upset that Grace was leaving us in the dark about The Colossal Lands and its dangers. "Maybe she's working for LaCroiux too," I added.

Phillip's eyes grew wide.

Then, I heard rustling behind me. Grace ran at me just as I turned around, pulled her sword on me and pinned me against the wall.

She held the sword at my face and yelled, "I would never side with that heartless, wicked monster! He has taken everything from us. EVERYTHING!" She spit those words in my face, like a fire-breathing dragon.

"Grace, I...I didn't. You wouldn't," I stammered as the blade of her sword shined in my eye.

"Grace, let her go," Whizzy commanded. He pointed his wand at the back of her head. "Don't make me do it, Grace." His voice was now much softer.

"We need to stick together," Phillip croaked. "This is exactly what Cragon and LaCroiux want...us fighting each other."

Grace continued to stare me down. She had so much hatred in her once beautiful eyes. Now they seemed dark and dangerous.

"Grace, I'm sorry," I cried. It was a simple gesture, but I truly meant it.

Suddenly, the elf changed, like a light switch had been turned on, and her eyes instantly flashed back to their original beauty. She released her strong grip on my fur, and pulled the sword back to her side. Grace slowly walked away. Her rage was now shame.

"Forgive me," she pleaded and then ran away into the grass beyond our safety trench.

I slid down the dirt wall where she had pinned me and sat on the ground. I began to cry.

"Rachel, are you okay?" Phillip asked as he reached out in an attempt to console me.

"Why did I say that? I knew she couldn't be a traitor." I continued to cry.

Whizzy shook his head in disappointment, and then went out after Grace.

I was exhausted. Phillip sat down beside me and wrapped his arms around me. His chest pressed up against my ear. It wasn't long before the steady beating of his heart put me to sleep.

My sleep was restless. Phillip told me that I thrashed around like I was still fighting in the battle. He said that I kept calling out for my grandpa. I don't remember much from my dreams; however, Grandpa Whizzenmog being buried in the snow was one of them.

I was startled awake by the vivid image of Grandpa falling beneath the snow. His dirty gray paw being the last thing I saw. When I awoke, I was still crying and Phillip was still with me.

He looked concerned.

"Phillip," I gasped while trying to catch my breath. It felt like I had just run a hundred miles.

He smiled back at me and then rubbed his webbed hand across my furry cheek to wipe away the tears.

My head throbbed between my eyes. It made my vision blurry. I searched around the trench attempting to focus my sight. It was very bare, mostly dirt with a few roots and a pile of grass and rocks next to Phillip where he had been building a slingshot for Grace.

Grace? I thought.

Phillip's expression changed. He looked concerned.

I again searched the trench for Grace and my brother before asking the question.

"Phillip, where is my brother?"

SPIKY GREEN BLOB

14

"Where is Whizzy, Phillip?" I screamed at him.

"He is with Grace, Rachel. Relax. Please!" He pleaded with me.

By now, I was pacing around the trench, huffing and crying. It wasn't very pretty.

Phillip tried to calm me down, but every time he tried I would just grow more worried...and frustrated.

"We have to go after them, Phillip!" I demanded.

"I'm not going out there?" Phillip gulped.

"What? Why not?" I demanded an answer. "He's your best friend!"

"Yes, and he has a bodyguard," the red-eyed tree frog reminded me.

I paced around for a few more seconds running scenarios of how to save Whizzy in my head.

I could make wings out of blades of grass and fly to him.

Maybe I can dig an underground tunnel below him and when I do he'll fall in the hole and I can drag his whinny butt back here.

"That's a good one," Phillip laughed.

"Are you reading my mind?" I barked.

"Or how about I use a slingshot and shoot Phillip's big head into the air as a signal so Whizzy can find his way back!"

"That's not funny," Phillip replied with a sour look on his green face.

"Stop reading my mind!" I growled in my head.

"Then talk to me, Rachel," Phillip pleaded still using his powers of telepathy. "I just want to help you."

"I know, Phillip. I'm sorry."

Just then Whizzy burst through the tall blades of grass and tumbled down the side of the trench. He rolled to a stop at Phillip's feet.

"Hey, Whizzy...where's Grace?" Phillip calmly asked.

Whizzy was breathing very heavily.

"You jerk!" I yelled; then I punched him in the shoulder.

He was terrified. I hadn't seen him that afraid since he hit Billy Lawton in the family jewels with a dodge ball in gym class back in the seventh grade.

"Run!" Whizzy shouted at me.

Funny...that was what he did in gym class too.

"Whizzy...wait what's wrong?" I pulled on his arm trying to keep him from running away.

"Let go?" He yelled and pointed his wand at me. He was crazed.

My heart began thumping. I couldn't believe it, but my own brother was about to zap me with his wand. I was frozen with shock. Whizzy's bright blue eyes grew wide, and his mouth opened exposing his sharp front teeth. His face was frightening. The tip of his wand began to light up. I started to yell. Phillip did too. Before I could react, a hot white flash zoomed past my head and exploded behind me. Phillip slammed into my brother knocking them and me to the ground.

"No, don't eat me!" Whizzy screamed.

"Eat you?" I said with a mouth full of dirt.

When I turned around, I squealed in terror.

Above us was the biggest, fattest, spiky green blob I had ever seen.

"What is that?" I yelled to Phillip.

"I don't know," he replied with no emotion, like he was in a trance.

We untangled ourselves from one another and ran. A ground-shaking thud rumbled through the dirt below us. I stumbled and fell. Phillip did too. Whizzy somehow managed to keep running.

"Whizzy! Don't leave me," I yelled.

My brother skidded to a stop and stared at the green blob with hundreds of sharp spikes like a porcupine, jutting out from its body inching toward us.

A rush of wind echoed in my ears. I rolled over onto my back to see Grace Tallon flying into the trench on a glider made from roots and flower petals.

"You have to be kidding me," I said in amazement.

The Elven warrior landed hard on her feet between the hairy blob monster and me. She drew her sword to protect me and put out her hand.

I grabbed hold and she pulled me up.

"Thanks," I said gratefully, now standing next to her and gripping my wand. "Grace...what is that?"

She replied, "That is Kiefer."

"Excuse me?"

"Kiefer the Caterpillar," Grace replied with a smile.

I stopped for the first time and looked up at the sloppy green blob moving slowly across the dirt. Upon its face were two enormous flat circles for eyes and nothing else. The long spikes sticking out all over its body were more like hairs. It was a scary image, like something out of a Halloween nightmare.

"A caterpillar?" I said hoping not to sound stupid. "We are running away from a bug."

"Well, this bug just might eat you for dinner," Grace frankly stated.

"But don't caterpillars only eat plants?" Phillip asked.

I waited for Grace to answer as Kiefer made his approach. She was taking too long to answer.

"Well?" I shouted.

"Maybe they do where you are from, but in Mistasia Kiefer eats whatever he wants to," Grace replied, now pointing the tip of her sword directly at Kiefer the Caterpillar, who had apparently slithered his way across the trench to dine on us. It was obvious he didn't avoid too many opportunities to snack.

"I don't wanna be that thing's dinner!" The thought of being swallowed up by this smelly, disgusting blob was not how I wanted things to end.

My wand began to glow.

"Rachel! Don't fire," Grace commanded. "Let me talk to him."

"Talk to him...he doesn't have a mouth!" Whizzy snarked.

The tension was heavy on us all. What if she couldn't talk Kiefer into not eating us like treats...would our magic be strong enough to stop something so big. He was like a house, a very green and disgusting house.

"Kiefer, in the name of Princess Merran Cadieux, I order you to not eat us," Grace strongly protested the monster's hungry impulses.

Kiefer lurched upward pushing its massive head skyward. Underneath the caterpillar's round head I could see its grotesque mouth with tiny teeth and hairs protruded out. It was sickening. I felt my stomach flop. Then the noises began. It was a strange array of sounds between a belly growl and a blender spinning at high speed.

We all took a few steps back.

Grace Tallon moved to protect us. She was only a few feet from the green beast when it bellowed again.

"Kiefer, you leave me no choice," she yelled.

"This is crazy," I overheard Whizzy whispered to Phillip.

Grace pulled her sword back, and widened her stance, preparing to strike the caterpillar in the abdomen.

Kiefer lunged at the Elven warrior and she stabbed him in the belly. The caterpillar let out a horrifying high-pitched squeal and flopped onto the dirt. Dust flew into the air blocking our sight.

Phillip grabbed my wrist. I reached out for Whizzy and found his paw. The three of us waited for the dust to settle. Grace's silhouette emerged in the dust cloud. It began to grow darker as the dirt settled back to the ground. Lying next to her was the giant caterpillar named Kiefer.

"She did it," Phillip called out in amazement.

Whizzy and Phillip gave each other a 'high-five' like they had just saved us.

I ran over to Grace and hugged her. "Thank you for coming back, Grace. I am so sorry."

"You were really awesome," Whizzy said to Grace.

Phillip and I began to laugh.

"What?" Whizzy said, giving us both a peculiar expression.

"Okay, so what's for dinner?" A nasally voice overtook the laughter.

We all looked up to see the large green caterpillar hovering directly above us. A string of spit hung from its mouth.

Phillip and I screamed. Whizzy made some strange noise...I don't know if it was him crying or wetting himself, but it was definitely not manly.

"Good job, Kiefer. You really got them," Grace smiled.

"Wha-u-sa?" Whizzy couldn't fully express himself. He had the dumbest look on his face as he tried to figure out what had just happened.

"This was a trick?" I blurted out.

"Kiefer is the one friend I know in The Colossal Lands," Grace explained. "I went out to find him. If anyone can help us escape unharmed, it's him."

"But he's a caterpillar," Phillip stated the obvious, sounding as confused as Whizzy appeared.

My brother still stared ignorantly at Kiefer, possibly hoping that he would magically disappear at any moment.

"Yes, and you're a frog. I like this game. Who's next?" Kiefer's large eyes now directed themselves to me. "And you're a fox." He continued.

"Yeah," I uncomfortably responded. This was quickly becoming one of the top 'strange moments' in my life...right up there with being dragged to another world by a talking snake.

"So he's not going to eat us?" Whizzy finally spoke looking for clarification on the current situation. His right eye began to twitch slightly.

I knew that wasn't a good sign. It meant that my brother was going to either explode in a rage or fart, and neither would be very pleasant right now.

"Oh, no!" Kiefer the Caterpillar responded. "Foxes give me bad gas."

"Oh, Whizzy this guy's right up your alley," I snidely remarked. "Wait a minute. When did you get a sense of humor?" I asked Grace.

She smiled. "I guess I've spent too much time with your brother," She jokingly responded.

"So when do we eat?" Kiefer asked again.

"If he is gonna protect us, we'd better feed him before he slims down. So where do we find a six-foot cricket?" Whizzy joked.

SORCERER'S NEW APPRENTICE

15

I haven't had too many normal moments in the past six months of my life, so a sixty-foot talking green caterpillar is just another oddity in what had become my irregular teenage life.

It had already been two days since we arrived back in Mistasia at the banks of Red River, which gave us eight remaining days to stop King Cragon, and return to Greenville before our parents came back home.

Grace and Whizzy had designed and built this amazing wheeled wagon using grass, roots, flowers, tree bark...basically anything found in the forest, and magic. We had fastened it to Kiefer allowing him to pull us along behind him. Grace stood on the great caterpillar's back weaving between the hairy spikes.

The trip was very slow moving. Kiefer wasn't necessarily the quickest moving bug. So we had to be patient, which wasn't working out well for me. The more time I had to sit and think the sadder and more distraught I became. I felt a weakness throughout my body.

All three of us had a weakness. They came from emotions, which I guess is pretty common at our age, but it had a different effect on each of us; Phillip's was confidence. In Greenville he was bullied and weak. He would let people put him down. Whizzy's was his temper. Being small all his life had made him angry and resentful. That turned into something almost uncontrollable lately. He could just explode at any given time. Mine had always been my lack of focus, just like in school. My parents always told me I was smart, but I just needed to study more. My grandpa had stressed the importance of keeping myself focused; it allowed me to gather my strength and increase my power as a witch.

I missed my grandpa so much. The image of his paw in the snow just kept replaying in my mind.

"Rachel?" Phillip sat down next to me and smiled.

I struggled to return a smile.

"Whizzy and I have been planning out an attack on the castle. Do you want to hear it?" Phillip eagerly explained.

An uncomfortable laugh escaped me. It was the only way I could keep from crying. "Phillip, not now."

"Oh...well, okay. Maybe later then," He got up and moved across the small-wheeled wagon to sit next to Whizzy.

Phillip leaned over and whispered something to my brother. Whizzy's face curled up in anger when he finished explaining that I didn't want to hear their plan.

"So you have a better idea, sis?" Whizzy challenged. "Are we too stupid?"

"Whizzy, not now."

My brother wondered why the girls at school never talked to him...this was why. He just doesn't understand them. Phillip wasn't much better, but at least he tried.

"Whizzy, I'm sorry, but I just can't handle that right now. I need to rest. We'll go over your plan after I wake up, okay?" I bargained with him, hoping to calm him down so I could rest.

He smiled, signaling he was pleased, so I immediately closed my eyes. I could feel the wagon rolling up and down over the uneven ground below. We swayed side to side slightly, but enough to make me feel uneasy. The horrid smell of sweaty gym socks and rotten milk hung in my snout. It rolled back to us from Kiefer. He was disgusting. I don't know how Grace could stand the smell from up there. I tried to relax, but every time I came close to falling asleep, something would wake me.

First, Phillip and Whizzy yelled when they watched a flying bug swallow another bug whole in mid flight. Next, we rocked so hard it tossed me up in the air, and I landed hard onto my stomach in the middle of the wooden wagon. Then, Whizzy belched. I don't think I even have to explain anymore, but those two knuckleheads giggled for like an hour afterward. Finally, Philllip and Whizzy fell asleep and it had grown quiet and peaceful enough that I drifted off myself, but not for long.

I awoke to absolute mayhem. An explosion had tossed the wagon sideways causing the three of us to fall out. I landed on Phillip, with his amphibian foot in my face. My heart nearly leapt from my chest.

Kiefer was thrashing around and making horrific high-pitched noises. Whizzy and I placed our paws over our sensitive fox ears. Phillip hopped up.

"Phillip!" I yelled and pulled him back down just as a bright red blast scorched the wheel off our wagon, sending it zipping across the field behind us, decapitating the tops of the tall blades of grass.

Phillip placed his hands around his neck realizing that could have been him. He gulped, "Thanks, Rachel."

We scrambled to find Grace in the commotion. When we found her, she pulled her sword out and sliced through the ropes holding the wagon to Kiefer. The giant caterpillar, once freed, began to roll to the left toward whatever attacked us.

Grace led us into the thick grass. She had stowed her sword, but now held her bow and arrow at the ready.

My brother and I joined her with our wands.

"Grace, do you mind?" Phillip pointed at her sword. "I'd like to use that."

Grace gladly handed over her sword, and ducked down as low as possible.

I joined her along the dirt-covered forest floor. "What do you see, Grace?" I asked knowing her Elven sight would allow her a much better view of the situation than mine.

Kiefer rolled back to the right as he took a direct hit to the side. The red-hot blast scorched his thick green skin, turning it black. The hairy spikes fell to the ground where he was burned. Our giant caterpillar friend roared and fired back, launching a series of spikes from his body like missiles into the air.

It went silent.

I took a deep breath. Had Kiefer struck our attacker? I attempted to stand up when Grace grabbed me.

"Wait," she spoke to me telepathically. "It is an elf," Grace spoke with astonishment.

"LaCroiux?" I whispered.

She shook her head. Grace squinted her eyes to see across the opening.

The broken wagon lay on its side smoldering in front of us, making it hard to see. Kiefer huffed in disgust. The black spot on his side began to ooze a white puss. In only a few seconds, the puss began to sizzle and bubble around the black wound. It quickly ate away and dissolved the wound until Kiefer's side was completely healed.

"That was amazing," Whizzy whispered, still aware that we were trying to not be found.

No, that is disgusting. I thought.

Suddenly, Grace bolted up and out through the grass into the open, with her arrow drawn.

"Whizzy," I yelled as my brother followed.

Grace let the arrow loose just as a small masked figure burst through the thick green blades of grass on the other side. The figure deflected the arrow causing it to glance off its shoulder.

Whizzy reacted, "Helar!" A light blue ray of light illuminated the darkened forest and covered the small figure's body.

The masked goon placed his arms in front of his body and pulled his knees to his elbows. A shield emerged, protecting him from Whizzy's freezing spell.

Grace fired again, but it slammed into the shield too and snapped in half.

Suddenly, our attacker landed on the ground, tumbled over and punched toward us with his fist, but didn't strike anyone. A wave of light jumped from his extended fist and knocked Whizzy and Grace to the ground.

Kiefer took a chance to protect Grace. He fired three more spikes. The masked figure dodged each, performing flips and jumps; it was amazing.

"Atar," Whizzy angrily fired another spell causing roots to burst through the dirt and wrap themselves around our enemy.

The mysterious enemy struggled to escape, but each second another root would grab hold.

Phillip and I joined Grace and Whizzy. We all stood together as the masked figure stood between Kiefer and us along the narrow trail.

"Who are you?" Grace commanded.

No response. The roots had covered the entire body of our attacker from its neck to knees.

"Don't let go," Grace said to Whizzy.

"I've got it," my brother proudly replied.

Phillip grabbed my paw. I didn't even realize at first, until I felt the cool dampness from his skin. A smile moved across my face.

"Who are you?" Grace shouted louder.

The captured figure refused to respond.

I was done playing games. I blasted the mask off to reveal the face of a young Elven man with oddly cut black hair and evil green eyes.

"Javid?" Grace said with disappointment.

"You know him?" I asked.

"Yes." Grace replied. "He is my brother."

MEET THE GRIMMIADS

16

"Your brother?" Whizzy shouted, causing the roots tied around Javid Tallon to loosen.

I quickly intervened and strengthened the magical hold around the evil elf.

"How could you?" Grace asked. She raised her bow and pointed its arrow directly at her brother's heart.

"Grace, don't," I attempted to reason with her.

I could see her rage beginning to overflow. Grace's usually steady hands were shaking, her voice different, softer, like she was ashamed to speak.

"You have disgraced our family, Javid. You will be banished from Mistasia," Grace stated as a tear rolled down her cheek.

"You are wrong, sister. I am not going anywhere. I work for the true ruler of Mistasia. It is you that will be banished," Javid scolded.

"He works for LaCroiux?" Phillip asked in an attempt to keep up.

"Maybe he is under a spell?" I whispered to Grace. "LaCroiux could be controlling him."

Javid began to laugh.

Grace gritted her teeth. "No. That's impossible."

"It has to be," I began when Grace interrupted.

"NO!" Grace shook her head in defiance.

"Elves are too strong willed for sorcerers to use their powers on them," Grace explained. "My brother acts of his

148

own will." Grace lowered her bow and arrow and walked away briskly.

I followed her. "Grace, stop. Wait. Why would he betray your family like this? Wait. Grace!" I yelled her name.

She finally stopped, but before she could speak, her brother attacked.

I had been controlling the spell that held Javid captive, but when I turned to walk after Grace, I forgot about the spell, which allowed the roots to weaken.

"Arrrhhh!" Sorcerer LaCroiux's new apprentice bellowed, as he broke free.

We had no time to react. He caught us with our guards down. Javid summoned the winds. They whipped in through the grass, bending the blades to the ground. Javid Tallon spun like a tornado and rose into the air. The winds raced passed us so quickly that they began to pull us toward him.

I tried to call out to my brother, but nothing came out, like something had placed my voice on mute. The wind roared in my ears as if I stood next to a jet engine.

Javid raised his arms into the air and then everything stopped. The winds vanished and Javid came crashing down. When he landed, the ground shook like an earthquake, knocking us all down. Then the ground beneath Javid Tallon split. The crack grew and spread across the field in an instant.

Suddenly, the dirt beneath us let loose and collapsed. We all fell into the darkness below.

I screamed as I tumbled into the unknown. It didn't last long...only a few seconds before we landed nearly twenty feet below the surface. Phillip and Whizzy were only a few feet away from me. Grace managed to land on her feet, as did her brother.

We began to gather ourselves. Javid and Grace were in a standoff. They were in the center of the hole we had fallen into and the light from above shone on them like a spotlight for everyone to see.

"Are you quick enough to hit me? Your arrow won't be able to pierce my shield," Javid challenged his sister. "Come on, Grace. Shoot. Do it!" He taunted her.

Grace pulled her bow back further than I had ever seen. She gripped it so tightly that her skin began to turn whiter than usual.

"You aren't even worth it," Grace replied. "I should have known you wouldn't be able to resist his temptation. You were always weak, Javid."

A few small rocks fell into the hole from above.

"Grace, I'm alone up here." The nasally voice of Kiefer the Caterpillar called down to her.

"Oh, no," Whizzy gasped.

"Kiefer back up," I shouted as the very large and heavy caterpillar hung dangerously over the side of the hole that we had all just fallen through. Kiefer was teetering on the edge and about to fall in on top of us.

Javid's wicked smile grew when he saw our friend hanging above. The Elven sorcerer swung his arm across the ground gathering rocks and stones in one swipe and launched them toward Kiefer.

"Run!" I yelled.

The rocks collided with the ground beneath Kiefer, causing it to crumble. The big green blob slipped and plummeted down toward us.

The crash was tremendous. It sounded like 500 drums banging in unison. My head rang so much my eyes rolled in my head like dice.

A dust plume rose into the air making it impossible to see. I just heard screaming and yelling. The commotion was startling. My heart was racing a million miles a minute. The dirt flying around caused me to cough.

When the dust settled, Kiefer's massive body occupied most of the area we had fallen into and Javid Tallon had disappeared.

Phillip was hurriedly tossing rocks and dirt aside like he was digging for buried treasure. That was when I heard him yell.

"Whizzy!"

My brother was trapped under the sixty-foot caterpillar that had just crashed down on top of us.

I ran to help Phillip.

"Whizzy. Whizzy!" my voice sounded strange. I just kept yelling frantically until I reached Phillip.

"What!" My brother snapped as he too, feverishly dug in the dirt under Kiefer.

"Oh, Whizzy, you're okay!" I hugged him

He pushed me away, "Get off of me!" He growled.

I looked to Phillip for an answer as to why my brother was being so rude.

"Grace," was all he replied.

Suddenly, I realized that not all of us had made it out. Grace and her brother Javid must have both ended up underneath Kiefer.

"Grace!" Whizzy excitedly yelled just before he dove into the small hole he and Phillip had dug beneath the large green caterpillar. "Phillip, grab my feet!" His muffled voice called.

Phillip began to pull at my brother's feet. I helped too. Each of us yanked on Whizzy's stinky paws. We dragged him out and he emerged clutching Grace's dirt-covered body with him.

"Is she breathing?" I asked Whizzy.

He placed his ear over her small Elven mouth.

"No!" He yelled.

Whizzy immediately began to resuscitate her. He pushed on her chest and then leaned in to breathe into her mouth. Just as his lips reached hers, Grace's eyes shot open.

She pushed Whizzy away, "What are you doing?" Grace demanded in a weak voice. She had a green-colored liquid running down her forehead and arm.

"You are injured, Grace," Phillip pointed to her forehead.

She reached up and touched the green blood coming from her head. The Elven warrior stood up. She looked very dizzy.

"Where is he?" Grace asked about her brother. The injured elf fell to her knees and spit blood.

"We think he's trapped under, Kiefer," Phillip explained.

Grace laughed for a second before spitting blood again.

Whizzy reached out to console her, but she swatted at him.

"Leave me alone. I am fine," the proud elf claimed as she attempted to stand up a second time. Once again, she stumbled to her knees and grabbed at her head.

"What do we do?" Phillip asked me.

"When did I become a doctor?" I harshly responded. "We've gotta get outta here."

How are we going to get back up there? I thought. Wherever we were was quite dark, except for the spot in the middle where Kiefer lay. I couldn't even see the walls.

My fox ears could hear many sounds; dripping water on something metallic, a whirring similar to mother's dishwasher, and scratching.

"Kiefer, where are we?" I asked the one creature that lived in these lands.

"The Grimmiad Tunnels," he replied in a pained voice.

"Are you okay?" I asked after realizing he was in pain.

"Something is stabbing me in the gut. It really hurts, Rachel the Fox," the big green blob whined.

I walked up to Kiefer's face and placed my hand out to comfort him. His eyes widened as he roared in agony, causing me to be tossed onto my back.

"It's raining," Whizzy crassly remarked.

"I don't think this is rain, Whizzy," Phillip said as he whipped the liquid from his froggy face.

"It's blood," Grace shouted. "Kiefer!" she cried out.

Kiefer's large head slumped. Then the great big bug let out a moan.

"What's happening to him?" I shouted to Grace Tallon.

Just then my question was answered as the wicked sorcerer emerged from Kiefer's midsection. He was covered in liquid too. His hair matted to his small head.

"Grace!" the enraged Javid Tallon called out to his sister. He punched the ground sending a wave of dirt directly at her.

She tried to leap away but was too late. The dirt whipped her legs, sending her flying through the air. When she landed, her bow slid to me. I grabbed it.

Javid quickly focused his evil little eyes on me. Running up the side of Kiefer's limp body, the elf sprung into the air soaring over my head and landing behind me. One quick punch landed in my chest when I turned around to face him. I flew backward and bounced off Kiefer.

I was unconscious for only a few minutes after hitting my head. When I awoke, I remembered seeing Grace when I lifted my head. She was too badly injured to continue to fight. Whizzy and I would have to battle her brother without her.

Phillip, get Grace away from here. I spoke in my head, hoping he would listen.

The green frog's glowing red eyes spotted me in the dimly lit tunnel. He dashed to Grace and swept her up off the ground. She didn't fight...she could barely move. Phillip leapt up and over our fallen friend, Kiefer, and disappeared.

Javid tried to stop him, by whipping stones from the ground, barely missing.

I pointed my wand at my target and attempted to hit Javid Tallon with a spell to slow him down, but he narrowly escaped.

The fleet-footed elf danced around, dodging each blast Whizzy and I cast at him. Javid was far faster than anything we had ever seen before...even faster than Grace.

He began to run circles around us. Whizzy and I stood back to back as the elf whirled around us so quickly that he spun up a funnel of dust. We were trapped.

Whizzy began to randomly fire spells into the funnel of dirt hoping to hit his target. Luckily, one did. Javid tumbled and crashed into the wall.

"Nice shot, Whizzy," I exclaimed.

My brother spun his wand in his paw like a drumstick.

"It only took twenty shots," I joked.

Javid pushed himself up to one knee. He was breathing very heavily. Green blood trickled from his bottom lip.

"That was a lucky shot," Javid warned. "You will not be so fortunate again." He started toward us.

In the distance a low rumble began.

The fuming sorcerer's apprentice hesitated at the new noise.

"Is this some trick?" He blasted.

Whizzy and I looked at each other with confusion. We had no idea what was making the noise either.

The rumbling grew louder. Stones and pebbles at my feet began trembling to the rhythm.

"Whizzy?" I called to my brother, hoping he wasn't as scared as I was. One look answered my question. My brother's eyes were huge, like he had just seen a ghost.

Even Javid had turned his back to us, looking into the darkness of the tunnel.

"Which one of you is doing this?" He yelled in fear.

The rumble sounded like a marching of footsteps. It was shaking the entire tunnel now.

I grabbed Whizzy's arm and pulled, tugging him toward Kiefer. We used his body to shield us from whatever was coming up the tunnel at us. Just then I remembered that I had sent Phillip and Grace in that direction only a few minutes earlier.

"Grace and Phillip," I gasped.

"What did you do, Rachel?" Whizzy blamed me for sending them fleeing into the dark and dangerous tunnel.

"How could I have known? It didn't look much safer here!" I shouted at him.

Then the noise completely stopped. It was eerily quiet. I could hear the wind blowing through the hole above us. I was more scared now. The silence was torture.

Whizzy and I held our wands across our chests and our backs against the now brownish-yellow skin of our lifeless caterpillar guide. Kiefer's color was fading.

"Where is that stupid, elf?" Whizzy peeked out. "I can't see him."

"I'm more concerned about Phillip and Grace."

A strong hand reached around my waist and yanked me away from my brother.

"Whizzy," I called out.

"Chede!" an angry voice blasted from behind me.

I felt a chill in my throat. A puff of smoke escaped my mouth, like when I exhale in the winter air. I couldn't speak! My throat was frozen.

Twisting my body I caught a glimpse of my kidnapper. It was Javid, but he had covered his face with his hideous mask once again. Now up close I noticed the black mask was painted with red streaks, like blood ran down his face. It had two small rectangular holes for his eyes, and an opening for his mouth and chin. He continued to drag me out into the open.

Whizzy ran after us, but Javid tossed him aside with a gust of wind, like a crumpled up piece of paper. The sinister elf held me so tightly that my ribs began to hurt. It was difficult to breath and my vision was becoming blurry.

We stopped so that Javid could easily see into the tunnel, but there appeared to be nothing there.

"Show yourself!" The frightened little sorcerer exclaimed in his deepest voice. "Come out and fight me!" He barked.

A series of tiny yellow dots appeared in the distance. At first I thought it was the lack of oxygen to my brain, until Javid took a sharp deep breath. Then I realized he must have seen them too.

"What deception is this, witch?" He whispered into my ear.

But I couldn't answer. His spell made it so I was unable to talk. It didn't matter because Phillip and Grace were gone and

Whizzy was unconscious after bumping his head on the ground when Javid attacked him.

More tiny yellow dots appeared with each passing moment. There were hundreds. It was creepy. The hairs on my furry neck began to stand up.

"Are you afraid of me?" Javid Tallon challenged the yellow dots. "Show yourself!" He screamed.

That was when the rumble from before returned...this time it was even more thunderous.

Emerging from the shadows were hundreds of squatty, hairy humans. They ran towards us with axes and swords. More and more brutish creatures continued to escape the shadows of the tunnel and flood into the moonlight that shone in from above.

Javid released his grip on me. I fell to the ground gasping for air. The chill in my throat disappeared.

I felt helpless against these new creatures, but I quickly realized I didn't need to fear them.

THE GREEN GLOW

17

The small, hairy looking humans stampeded by me chasing after Javid Tallon. Sorcerer LaCroiux's brash apprentice scurried up the tunnel wall, like a spider, and burst into the night sky. He landed in The Colossal Lands above and disappeared from view.

A small, but thick-fingered hand appeared next to my face. I followed the short arm up to a dirt-covered and hairy smiling face. It appeared to be a very small man, who only came to my chest, with short and spiky, yet thick, coarse black hair.

"Thank you?" I said, not quite knowing what else to say.

"You are welcome, Rachel Whizzenmog," the gruff, yet obviously female, voice surprised me.

"You know my name?" I replied.

She laughed. "Yez, we know who yuz are...we have long zince been knowing the Whizzenmog family. We Grimmiads have fought many battlez with yuz. I Gellna Grimmiad."

"It is nice to meet you, Gellna. And thanks again for saving me. Have you seen my friends?"

"Friendz? Do yuz mean the elf and the frog?" She began to heartily roar.

The many Grimmiads surrounding her joined in with a short burst of raucous laughter. Then, they all suddenly stopped.

Whizzy was startled awake by the commotion. "Rachel!" He yelled like the battle was still going on.

It's a good thing that he has red fur, because I could tell he was embarrassed after noticing that we were not alone.

"What's going on, sis? Who are the dwarfs?" Whizzy joked.

"Grimmiads, Michael Whizzenmog!" Gellna forcefully responded.

"Sorry. I didn't know," Whizzy rolled his eyes at me. "What's a Grim-nod?" my brother whispered in my ear.

"You're an idiot!" I replied.

"What?" He shrugged his shoulders.

"Whizzy has this problem where he sometimes forgets to use his brain and his mouth runs amok," I explained to Gellna and the other Grimmiads. "I'm sorry to be in such a hurry, but we need to return to Cadieux Castle. Can you take us to our friends?"

"Yez, we will take yuz to them." Gellna began to lead the way when she stopped to place her hand on Kiefer's face.

She closed her eyes and began speaking in a language I didn't recognize.

"Short and funny. I like these people," Whizzy glibly spoke.

I swatted him in the chest.

"Castle ride soon yuz will have, Whizzenmogs," the Grimmiad leader declared as she rubbed Kiefer the Caterpillar's peaceful face.

She led us down the tunnel a short way to where Grace and Phillip were being protected by another swarm of Grimmiads.

"Phillip!" I ran and hugged him. I was so relieved to see him alive.

Whizzy just stood uncomfortably at Grace's feet not knowing if he should speak. It was then I realized that the last time they were together she awoke to him kissing her...sort of.

"Grace, are you okay?" Whizzy mustered up the courage to ask.

"I'm fine, Whizzy." She replied in discomfort.

"How are we going to get back to the castle now?" I asked referring to our Elven guide's injuries and Kiefer's passing. "Is there another way back to Cadieux Castle, Gellna?"

A vibrant smile came over her face. "Yuz will be in Caduz sooner than yuz realize," she boasted. "Coming event will make it so."

I had no idea to what she was referring, but Gellna Grimmiad had recently saved my life so I wasn't about to argue with her...and her hundreds of Grimmiad fighters so I sat down beside Phillip and waited.

The Grimmiads hustled about the tunnel. Some carried weapons and others food. They appeared to be gathering supplies.

"What do you think they are doing?" Whizzy snidely remarked, pointing at three peculiar-looking Grimmiads directly across from us.

One had a silver helmet on his head that covered his ears and nose. His fat cheeks burst out in front, and he was also missing a few teeth. The second had streaks of gray in his hair, which reminded me of our grandpa. Suddenly, I felt sad again. The third was rather thin and a few inches taller than the others. He was actually close to my brother's height. He had a very long braided beard and long hair that resembled tentacles in the back. His eyes were yellow, like his friends', but appeared sharper.

They huddled around a pile of axes, arrows and swords. The Grimmiad wearing the silver helmet pulled a thick, but short sword out from the pile and slashed it back and forth. It produced a strange sound as it cut through the air. The others chuckled, while he made a goofy face.

The bearded Grimmiad then grabbed an axe and swung it about like a baton twirler in a marching band, almost striking his friend in the head.

They all began to laugh again.

"It looks like they're trying to kill each other," Phillip replied. Then he started laughing and Whizzy joined him.

Grace and I gave each other an annoyed glance.

"We can't just wait here forever. I'm not even sure how many days we have left?" I was getting worried that we wouldn't return to Greenville in time...or with our grandpa.

"Six days," Phillip responded.

"How do you know that? Can you be absolutely sure?" I challenged.

"Yes. I am sure. We have had four sunsets since we arrived. One on our journey to the castle, another at the castle and now two here," Phillip explained.

We all looked at him like he was crazy.

"I can feel the moon," he added.

"You're mental!" Whizzy shouted. "Feel the moon. That is ridiculous."

"He is correct, Whizzy. I can feel the moon's power. It is nighttime," Grace Tallon replied.

"How is that possible?" I asked Grace. "Why would Phillip be able to feel the moon in the sky?"

"The tide!" Phillip muttered. "The tides control the water, and water gives me strength."

"So?" Whizzy blasted, not understanding anything his best friend was explaining.

"Do you ever pay attention at school?" Phillip snapped back. "The moon controls the levels of water. When it is up at night, the water levels rise due to gravity. So that must be why I can tell when the moon has risen even without being able to see it. Its control over water is like when I become stronger around water. That's the connection."

"I have no idea what you just said. There were words coming out of your mouth, but I only heard 'water'. The rest of it was kinda...not so much!" Whizzy jokingly replied.

"Whizzenmog, you must make your family proud," Grace jabbed.

I started laughing but then I noticed Phillip's eyes glued to something directly over my head.

"What?" I shouted afraid there was a giant spider dangling between my fox ears. The image of a sixty-foot spider jumped into my head.

Phillip pointed behind me. When I turned around, there were dozens of Grimmiads clustered together with their backs to us. A commotion rose from them. Phillip, Whizzy and I stood up to see.

A bright green light shimmered on the tunnel wall. The strange light was getting brighter and began swirling around like the water draining in a toilet.

The rushing wind sounded like a vacuum cleaner stuck on a carpet floor. A flash leapt into the once dark underground tunnel.

The Grimmiads erupted in cheers. Standing amongst them was an image I never thought I would see again.

A smile beamed across my face. I gasped at the sight of the gray fox towering over the Grimmiads.

"Grandpa!" Whizzy spoke in disbelief.

Grandpa had returned. He was clutching his wand and the powerful gem that had allowed him to escape the snow outside Cadieux Castle, the Last Emerald.

THE LAST EMERALD

18

Grandpa Whizzenmog hunched over in pain. The Grimmiads caught him before he fell. The short but strong dwarves helped Grandpa walk over to us. He used them like crutches.

I was so excited. My emotions swamped me. I started hopping around like a five year old on Christmas morning ready to open presents. My eyes welled up with tears. I wanted to hug him so badly but was afraid to touch him. He looked so fragile.

"Rainer Whizzenmog, what took you so long?" Grace Tallon interrupted my joy. She sternly glared at him.

"I am sorry, my dear." My grandpa rolled his eyes at me. "She thinks this is easy," he whispered.

"I heard that, Rainer," the Elven warrior replied.

The old fox just smiled. The Grimmiads helped him to the ground, where he sat beside me. He exhaled deeply like a huge weight had just been lifted from his shoulders.

I watched as he turned the gem into a bracelet by waving his wand around it in a circular motion. He struggled to place it around his wrist.

"Let me help you," I said as I reached out to grab the green bracelet.

Grandpa Whizzenmog pulled it away quickly and then winced in pain.

I was shocked. Why would he pull it away from me? I wasn't going to steal it.

My grandpa quickly noticed my expression, and responded with, "Rachel, I know you just want to help, but...I cannot allow you to put yourself in such danger. I am sorry, my dear."

We sat in silence for a few seconds. At that time, I noticed that the Grimmiads had once again resumed their strange behaviors from before. They tested out weapons on each other, laughing all the while.

These guys are weird. I thought.

I searched for Phillip to see if he was possibly listening to my mind again, but he wasn't. He and Whizzy had begun playing with the Grimmiads' weapons as well.

I wondered how long it would be before one of them sliced off a limb. My money would be on Whizzy...doing it to Phillip.

I was just about to ask my grandpa if we could use magic to reattach body parts when he suddenly began telling me about the Last Emerald as if I had asked him a question.

He had a guilty look on his face when he spoke, "This is a magical stone, Rachel." The green bracelet stuck out against his gray-colored fur. He bent his wrist to show me...as if I hadn't seen it before or watched him place it on his wrist seconds before. "In Greenville, it is only a visual piece of art, nothing more." He continued to explain. "However, here in Mistasia it has many powers. You have already seen some of what the beholder of this gemstone is capable of...but it has far greater powers than anything I have demonstrated." Grandpa was now speaking in a whisper and had leaned in uncomfortably close even for a family member. "In this world, an emerald like this could be used to change the face of everything we see, control all the creatures, and reshape the world. If Cragon Cadieux is allowed to possess this emerald, Rachel...Mistasia would be lost forever."

The sudden flash of thoughts in my head unsettled my stomach. Imagining what Cragon Cadieux could do with a magical weapon like that. It was horrifying. The pain and suffering would be so wide spread that Mistasia would be destroyed.

"What do we do? How can we keep him from stealing it?" I asked in a panic.

"We will have to destroy it," Grace Tallon interjected.

I saw my grandpa's face contort in pain as he shifted uncomfortably next to me, but he didn't respond.

"Is that possible?" I asked, looking between Grace and my grandpa for a response.

"He could do it!" Grace answered before Grandpa was able to catch his breath and respond.

Grandpa Whizzenmog and Grace Tallon silently glared at one another.

"What do you mean he could do it? Can you do that?" I found myself feeling a lot like Whizzy right now as my frustration level grew with each new question I asked.

"I take it you haven't told them yet, Rainer?" Grace spoke with an odd tone in her voice. It sounded like sarcasm.

Grandpa attempted to swallow and then replied. "Yes." He wouldn't look at me.

"Yes? Yes, what? To which question? Is that possible? Can you do it? What?" I began shouting, drawing my brother's and Phillip's attention as well as a few hundred Grimmiads.

Suddenly, our once private conversation had developed into a large-scale meeting.

Grandpa leaned close to me and whispered, "To both."

I didn't exactly know how to take that. "If this emerald is so powerful and so dangerous if Cragon gets hold of it, then why haven't you destroyed it?" I sternly questioned my grandpa.

"There are many reasons, Rachel."

I waited for him to elaborate, but he didn't. "That's your answer? Many reasons? We are risking our lives for that?"

"What's going on, Rachel?" Whizzy finally joined in the conversation.

"Yeah, why are you so upset? I thought you'd be happy to see your grandpa alive," Phillip added while twirling a Grimmiad sword in his webbed hand.

"I did too," I replied and then stormed away.

I was furious. It seemed so selfish that he kept the emerald, like a trophy when destroying it would make Cragon so much easier to defeat. I spent the next few hours alone trying to understand my grandpa's reasoning. It didn't help. I couldn't.

Later that day, a commotion rose from the area of the tunnel where we had fallen in the day before from The Colossal Lands.

I ran back towards the hundreds of Grimmiads chanting and roaring in unison. Phillip, Whizzy, Grace and Grandpa were standing together behind the Grimmiads, watching them dance around. At the center of this celebration, was Gellna. She had her stubby arms raised above her head as she barked out unfamiliar words into the sky.

"Chun...ba...rune! Ramme...varoon!" The Grimmiad leader chanted repeatedly.

It was a few moments before I realized that directly behind the cluster of short, hairy Grimmiads was a large, dark brown pile of dirt.

"Did they bury, Kiefer?" I asked Phillip.

"They must have," he replied.

As the Grimmiads sang and danced in the tunnel, the rumbling grew.

"Did that just move?" I wondered out loud, referring to the pile of dirt.

"Ahhhh, I think so," Phillip answered, as he scratched between his big red eyes.

I watched intently as the massive lump of dirt shifted and stretched like something stuck inside a sack. Suddenly, it burst at the top. Liquid flowed out like a broken water balloon. A slimy colorfully winged creature emerged.

"What is that?" Whizzy shrieked like a frightened child. He stepped behind his best friend for protection.

I remember thinking he was acting like a pansy, but didn't get the chance to tell him before I realized something.

"Is that...?" I started.

"It can't be," Phillip defiantly replied.

"That's a freaking huge butterfly," I shouted.

"It's Kiefer," Grace responded.

"What?" Phillip, Whizzy and I yelled.

RUMBLING IN THE DISTANCE
19

"Now that is magical!" Grandpa
Whizzenmog boasted with a chuckle. He was
grinning widely. "Mistasian nature."

The Grimmiads continued to dance
around between the massive butterfly and
us that had suddenly emerged from the dirt
cocoon.

Kiefer spread his wings, which had
strings of slimy goo stretching from them to
his body. He flapped them, slopping the
gooey liquid all over the tunnel. The
Grimmiads were covered in Kiefer's slime,
like he had just sneezed upon them. The
Grimmiads only cheered louder.

Gellna Grimmiad began to grunt and
her followers did too.

Grace smiled as she looked up at the flying creature.

Kiefer was nearly as big as a jumbo jet but far more colorful. I couldn't wait to see him up close. I ran and Phillip followed. Dodging piles of slime, I dashed to our revived friend's side.

"Kiefer, you look amazing!" I shouted with joy. "I completely forgot that caterpillars turn into butterflies. This is amazing."

I began to examine his beautifully colored wings. The morning sunlight from above shone into the dark tunnel and directly on Kiefer. It made his wings shimmer. The colors swirled and spiraled around on his wings. Red turned to yellow and then green. Dozens of vibrant blue circles covered his wings too. His body was bright yellow now and fuzzy like a peach.

Phillip was rubbing Kiefer's furry side when the giant butterfly spoke in a deeper voice.

"Rainer Whizzenmog, we must move quickly. The evil sorcerer is headed our way."

"Thank you, Kiefer," Grandpa responded. He appeared worried.

"We will aid yuz, Rainer Whizzenmog," Gellna told our grandpa.

The gray fox bowed his head in response. He was standing in the center of a mass of followers.

Phillip, Whizzy, Grace and I were with him without a doubt. The Grimmiads had given their word to fight with us too, and now Kiefer had been reborn as a butterfly. We definitely had weapons at our disposal...and in this battle we wouldn't be as badly outnumbered as we had been at Cadieux Castle. Yet, I still felt sick to my stomach, like that nervous feeling I get when I have to take a math test...except when I answer incorrectly at school, an evil sorcerer doesn't zap me.

"We can use The Colossal Lands to our advantage," Grace spoke. "Kiefer and Gellna know these lands better than anyone."

"Yeah, this time we're gonna kick his butt!" Whizzy shouted.

The Grimmiads cheered!

I still felt sick.

"All right everyone, let's go!" Grandpa suddenly shouted, exciting the Grimmiads into a frenzy.

The little people began to scurry about the tunnel gathering weapons. Gellna shouted instructions to them as Grandpa called us together.

"Grace, in battle I want you to stay with Whizzy. Phillip, stick close to Rachel. We all will fly out on Kiefer. They won't be expecting that!" Grandpa explained with a sly smile.

Our grandpa leapt upon the great butterfly's back with the flick of his wand. A gust of wind lifted him skyward and safely landed him on Kiefer's fuzzy body.

"Cool," was my brother's simple response.

I was just glad the gust of wind was magic and not a fart like back in my parent's house.

Whizzy was next to join Grandpa. Then Phillip wrapped his arms around Grace, who was still sore from her battle with Javid, and leapt skyward with great force. A whoosh sound buzzed my ears as he jumped past. I took a deep breath and whispered, "Catapult." My body was flung upward. My heart began pumping so fast. Kiefer's brightly colored body whizzed past me, and then his wing and suddenly I was flying out of the Grimmiad tunnel and landing in the thick green grass of The

Colossal Lands. I had overshot my target because of my excitement.

Phillip called to me using his telepathy, "Rachel are you all right?" His voice resonated with fear in my head.

"Yeah...I just used too much magic," I replied with embarrassment as the ground around me began to tremble.

The rocks at my feet bounced around like the crowd at a concert. Wind gusts blew dirt into my face and through my fur. Kiefer emerged from the hole in front of me.

I ran and jumped onto his back as he rose. Phillip and Whizzy grabbed me. My right paw slipped on the butterfly's fur, causing me to dangle off his side. Whizzy struggled to hold on to me. I could feel his grip slipping.

"I can't hold her!" Whizzy yelled for help.

"Help me!" I screamed as Kiefer continued to climb into the air. I looked down and saw the long drop into the dark tunnel. "Whizzy!"

"Phillip, pull," my brother barked at his best friend.

"I am!" Phillip replied, as his voice trembled while he struggled to keep his grip on me.

My hand slipped from Whizzy's, causing my body to swing like a clock pendulum and slam into Kiefer's side.

"Rachel!" I heard my brother's voice.

My heart skipped a beat. I gasped at the sight of the drop to the green grass.

Suddenly, I felt a tug against my body like a pair of large hands wrapping themselves around me and lifting me up to place me down safely on Kiefer's soft fuzzy back.

When I looked up, Grandpa Whizzenmog smiled at me. "You are safe, my dear."

I hugged him so tightly. My grandpa had saved me. He hadn't panicked. He used his magical powers to pull me to safety. I was still mad at him about the emerald, but very glad he was here.

After my heart slowed back to normal, my eyes caught a glimpse of our future. In the distance was a massive field of waving green grass. It spread out far into the distance. As the grass swayed, black blurry images emerged...hundreds of them!

"Wolverines!" Whizzy growled as he pointed to the same figures I saw. "Look...see! In the grass,"

"I see them Whizzy!" I cracked back.

"What's that sound?" Phillip croaked.

A mechanical whirring shot up from the ground below and could be heard over the flapping of Kiefer's wings. Large chunks of grass were being cut down in strips to allow the Wolverine Army to easily pass through The Colossal Lands. The paths looked like cracks in the green fields and they all were coming directly toward us.

Grandpa instructed Kiefer to hover in one spot.

"What's our strategy, Whizzenmog?" Grace smugly questioned our leader.

"To stay alive!" The stern voice of Grandpa Whizzenmog replied.

A TANGLED WEB

20

That phrase, 'To stay alive', hung in my brain like a spider web in the corner of our basement. It dangled there swaying in the wind, unable to fall...catching every horrible thought I could possibly have about our impending battle.

"Right now, I wish I'd never come back!" Whizzy blurted out.

It was exactly what I was thinking...I just didn't have the courage to say it because we were all the hope that remained for all of Mistasia.

The Wolverine Army amassed in great numbers. Meanwhile, the Grimmiads were nowhere to be found. They had promised to help us, but I couldn't find them anywhere.

"This isn't looking very good," Phillip commented on the large number of enemy soldiers in the distance.

"How are they getting here?" Grace questioned.

"I have no idea?" Grandpa responded. He squinted his aged eyes in an attempt to see clearly. "Can you see anything, Grace?"

The Elven warrior focused her powerful eyes at the wolverines. "I can see flashes of light. Then they just appear in small groups."

"LaCroiux?" Grandpa growled.

"No, it's Javid!" Grace gritted her teeth in disgust.

"Who?" Grandpa asked.

"My brother."

"You have a brother?" Grandpa replied.

Grace nodded.

"And he works for LaCroiux?" Grandpa sarcastically questioned.

Grace tilted her head slightly and rolled her eyes. "Yes."

"So you're not gonna invite him over for dinner anytime soon," Grandpa cracked.

I smiled.

"No, but I'll give him something to eat," she replied clenching her fist.

"You'll get your chance," I added watching the Wolverine Army begin to move closer. "Where are the Grimmiads?"

"We can't wait much longer," Whizzy stated the obvious.

"Then we are going to have to stop them on our own," Grandpa calmly replied. "Grace, are you up to this?"

Grace nodded and grabbed an arrow from her backpack. "Just tell me when, Rainer."

"Good. I will go down and attack them from the ground using the grass as cover. I need the rest of you to take Kiefer and stop Javid from bringing anymore soldiers here," our leader commanded.

"Kiefer, down!" Grace ordered.

"Wait!" Grandpa shouted to stop the giant butterfly from descending. "I have another way down." He winked at me with a sly smile on his face.

"Wingadom," the crafty fox spoke as he flicked his wand toward his chest. Grandpa held his arms out stretched from his sides. Under his arms a glowing light began to form wings that attached from his hips to his wrists like a bat.

Grandpa ran to the end of Kiefer's body and leapt. I watched in fear as he plummeted to the ground. His arms were held out and wings bowed against the rushing winds. Just before hitting the ground, Grandpa lurched back causing the wind to catch his wings and pull him skyward again. The gray fox did a full circle in the air and landed squarely on his paws.

"That was freaking awesome!" Whizzy blurted out.

"You would have killed yourself," Grace taunted the reddish-colored fox.

"Look out," I heard Phillip croak from beside me.

He pointed down at my grandpa. Wolverines were closing in on him quickly, and Grandpa was unable to see them through the tall grass.

"Call to him, Phillip!" I shouted. "Use your powers."

Phillip used his telepathy to warn Grandpa. I helplessly watched from above as Kiefer began to fly away with us on his back. We were supposed to stop Javid from bringing more soldiers here, but I couldn't leave my grandpa alone. I stepped to the edge of Kiefer's back and prepared to jump when Phillip's damp webbed hands grabbed me and pulled me back.

"Stop! Let go! I have to help him!" I screamed.

"He told us to stop Javid, Rachel. He can handle them!" Phillip shouted back as he struggled to hold onto me.

Just then the first wolverine approached Grandpa.

I gasped as it swung its large sword.

A flash of light erupted from the ground, and the wolverine was flung through the air and down into the large dark hole to Grimmiad tunnel.

Grandpa used his wand like a sword to fend off two more wolverines. He slashed at one enemy and dodged the attack from the other. More and more wolverines converged on his position. Their thick black fur was beginning to overtake the green of the grass surrounding him. They used their machines to cut the grass to the ground. Now a large section had been destroyed around them. Grandpa stood in the middle with dozens of wolverines all around him. He was trapped.

"Kiefer go back!" I yelled.

Phillip didn't try to stop me this time. He watched in terror as Grandpa tried to fight them off.

A large wolverine stepped up through his brothers and approached the gray wizard fox. He was the tallest and most muscular wolverine I'd ever seen. He carried a club that resembled a tree.

Grace Tallon pulled back hard on her bow. She fired, missing the huge wolverine that prepared to attack Grandpa. It whizzed by and struck another black-haired beast, which fell to the ground in pain.

A loud roar erupted from the ground below. It was becoming harder to see and the sun had almost set. That was when a thundering noise began.

"A storm?" Whizzy said searching the clouds above.

There didn't appear to be any storm, but we knew that in Mistasia anything could happen and probably would. A tornado could instantly spring up out of one of the wolverine's rear-ends and I wouldn't be surprised.

A familiar voice grunted. It was Gellna Grimmiad as she burst from the hole in the ground behind my grandpa. She was riding a huge black spider with ugly yellow eyes.

"Oh, yeah!" Whizzy yelled as he pumped his fists with excitement. "Get 'em!"

The Grimmiads had kept their promise and emerged from their tunnel, riding large spiders. The Wolverine Army was no match for the arachnids.

Gellna rode up to Grandpa quickly. Her spider spit a web entangling the largest wolverine, which seemed small compared to the spiders.

Grandpa took the opportunity to strike and zapped his enemy. The wolverine froze and then crashed backwards to the ground. "Go! Stop Javid!" The angered fox called to us.

TALLON CHALLENGE

21

It was a frightening sight, like something out of a horror movie. Giant spiders scurried below...their glowing yellow eyes targeting their prey before shooting webs like nets, trapping wolverines in thick cocoons.

My heart was racing...partly because of the scene below and partly because my adrenaline was pumping. I felt strength surging through my body. The momentum had swung in our direction.

Kiefer swooped down. Flashes of light pointed us in the right direction to find Javid as the sun had completely set and nightfall had arrived.

Our butterfly friend moved in close and hovered above the flashing lights.

"Where is he?" Whizzy yelled over the flapping of Kiefer's wings.

The sorcerer's apprentice answered with a scorching fireball, before any of us could respond.

Kiefer howled in pain as the flame singed his belly.

"We're hit!" Grace announced.

Kiefer began to spin uncontrollably toward the ground. His left wing was ablaze. The wind rushed by my face, causing my whiskers to point to my ears.

I reached for Phillip's hand. He pulled me tightly into his chest as we braced for a crash landing. I closed my eyes and wrapped my arms around him too.

Just before smashing into the ground, we came to a halt. Kiefer's large body hung in the air as if strings from above were holding him.

"What happened?" Kiefer's strangely normal voice asked.

I opened my eyes to see my brother standing in the middle of Kiefer's furry back. His entire body shook as if he was cold, but it was very warm in The Colossal Lands.

"I...can't...hold...him," Whizzy struggled to speak.

Whizzy had stopped Kiefer from crashing.

"Set us down, Whizzy." I was very impressed, but knew that setting down an object this large wouldn't be easy.

We dropped suddenly. Kiefer bounced on the ground, tossing us into the air like ragdolls.

Phillip's hold on me was broken. He extended his webbed hand, but I couldn't grab hold. We separated and fell to opposite sides of Kiefer's body.

I landed on my back on Kiefer's wing, and slid backward to the soft grass below.

Grace was laying face down to my left. I wasn't able to see Phillip or Whizzy.

"Grace, are you okay?" I reached out to touch her arm. Grace didn't respond, but stood up and walked by me.

I chased after her. She didn't seem right. When I saw Kiefer's face I understood why. Javid Tallon was awaiting his sister on the other side. Before I could reach her, Grace pulled two arrows from her pack and drew them back in her bow. She pointed them at Javid.

Phillip and Whizzy were standing at Kiefer's wing, Phillip holding a Grimmiad sword and Whizzy pointing his wand at the evil little sorcerer.

"Drop them," Javid demanded. "Now!" he barked.

"No, Javid! Surrender; we have you!" Grace pleaded.

Javid smiled and raised his left hand.

"You underestimate me, Grace," Javid said.

"You can't control me, Javid!" Grace explained, as she believed her brother was trying to use his sorcery on her.

Her bow began to vibrate, causing her to fire her arrow, and she nearly clipped Whizzy.

"Hey, Grace, watch it!" Whizzy growled.

The Elven warrior's bow jumped from her hands and hung in the air.

"No, but I can control your weapon." Javid moved the bow and pointed it at Grace. An arrow leapt from her pack, entered the bow and drew back.

"Stop it," I screamed and pointed my wand at Javid.

"Don't point that at her!" Whizzy shouted.

The arrow's tip glimmered in the moonlight.

"As you wish, fox!" Javid snidely remarked and then abruptly turned the bow and arrow toward Phillip and Whizzy.

The evil elf taunted Whizzy. "You care for my sister, don't you Whizzenmog? Then maybe you'd take an arrow for her?"

"I'd rather not," Whizzy snarled.

Javid fired, but Whizzy deflected the arrow into the ground with a simple spell.

"You'll have to do better than that," Whizzy replied feeling very confident.

Javid zipped into action whirling around and crouching to the ground, holding out his left arm and swiping it across the ground. The grass turned bright white before Javid slammed his right hand down like a hammer, sparking the grass into a wall of flame that raced toward Phillip and Whizzy. The two best friends split in opposite directions to avoid the flames.

Grace reached out and placed her hand on her brother's shoulders. Javid spun around and wrapped the bow around her neck. He began to choke her as Grace struggled to free herself. They wrestled for a moment when I pointed my wand at Javid.

"You'll hit her!" He yelled. "You wouldn't want to do that would you, Whizzenmog?"

Whizzy and Phillip approached Javid from opposite sides. I held my wand as steady as possible. Javid appeared to be assessing his situation. His shady eyes shifted back and forth between all of us. Then he attacked Phillip, lifting him from the ground in a funnel of wind and tossing him at my brother. Phillip's large frog head slammed into Whizzy's furry white chest. They tumbled to the ground.

I took the opportunity to fire a spell at Javid's shoulder, hoping not to hit Grace. Her brother turned at the last moment and pulled Grace in front of my spell.

It hit her directly in the face. Her eyes crossed and closed. Her body slumped in Javid's arms. The crooked little elf smiled at me and then released his hold on Grace.

Javid backed away as I approached him with my wand now fixed on his heart. I gritted my teeth in anger.

"It's over, Javid. Give up!" I ordered.

Phillip and Whizzy joined me. Whizzy pointed his wand at Javid, too. Phillip held his Grimmiad sword.

"Three against one. Those are good odds for you. However, I am up for the challenge.

In the distance, I could still hear the patter of the spiders rumbling around. I heard the sound of webs shooting from the spinnerets of spiders like a laser in a sci-fi movie, and then the howling from another captured wolverine.

"Listen. Your army is losing!" Whizzy growled. "We have won!"

Javid started to chuckle. His bright white teeth emerged from his darkened face. "Not yet!" He zipped between us in a flash, knocking me to the ground.

Phillip and Whizzy chased after him.

When I got back up, I saw Phillip hopping around dodging Javid's attempts to burn him to a crisp. Whizzy just stood confidently with his right leg forward and his left leg back, like a swordsman, as he continually fired blasts.

"Stand still, you twerp!" Whizzy growled.

Javid stopped for a moment with a confused expression.

Phillip reacted and pounced, kicking the elf in the head. He landed on top of Javid.

"Yeah, Phillip!" Whizzy shouted with excitement.

I had joined them as we began to celebrate our accomplishment.

"Ahhhhh!" Javid screamed in anger. He clenched his fists.

Phillip's eyes grew. He knew whatever was about to happen wouldn't be good.

The sorcerer's apprentice smashed his fists into the ground, driving into the green-covered grass and flinging shavings into the air. The sheer force produced a crack of thunder. Javid used the momentum it produced to kick his legs up and knock Phillip from his chest. The little Elven sorcerer spun and landed with his feet wide apart and one hand on the ground. He exploded toward Whizzy who suddenly had a wide-eyed and panicked expression on his face.

"Oh crap!" Whizzy gasped.

Javid whistled past Whizzy, ran up the side of Kiefer jumping into the air. With his legs pointed skyward, Grace's brother held his hands extended over his head and fired two sonic blasts into the ground between Whizzy and me.

The ground began to distort. It resembled waves on the ocean until the ground began to spin. It happened all in a few seconds. I couldn't watch.

A familiar screech stabbed my ears. When I turned back around, a ten-foot tall portal spun directly in front of me and dozens of vampire bats swarmed the sky.

SUMMON THE SORCERER

22

Boom! That was the sound that Javid's feet made when he landed back on the ground. He had a wicked smirk like he had just won the battle.

I didn't agree! I showed him by casting a spell to wrap him up with blades of grass like an Egyptian mummy.

Javid wiggled like a worm in an attempt to free himself, but I wasn't letting him go.

Vampire bats continued to circle above us but didn't attack. They appeared to be waiting for something.

Grace rustled. She stood up in pain, holding her face. Blood trickled from her nostrils. She dabbed her fingers at the blood.

"Why am I bleeding?" Grace asked no one in particular.

"Ah...that was me," I answered.

She gave me a sour look.

"Your brother used you as a shield," I angrily defended myself.

It was only an instant, but that was all Javid needed. As I verbally battled his sister, I lost focus...just for a split second and Javid used that opportunity to break the magical binds with which I held him.

I tried to hold him off. I cast spell after spell. The grass blades reached out and grabbed hold, but Javid kept snapping them and pulling himself free.

It was chaos! The vampire bats dove into action. Goren swooped in and slashed at me. I ducked. That was all that Javid needed to free himself completely. He spun, creating a whirlwind. At that same moment, Grandpa Whizzenmog appeared behind

Whizzy. Debris from Javid's tornado slapped against his face.

I covered my eyes with my arm.

Phillip braced for the impact; Javid's wind funnel crashed into him flinging him like a sock into the air. I heard the sound of the air escaping his lungs as he bounced on the ground behind me.

My wand slipped from my hand and was sucked up into the vortex.

"NO!" I screamed.

Grace fired two arrows into the funnel, but nothing happened. It crept along, crackling like a flag whipping in the wind.

Goren continued to dive-bomb us, swooping down and just missing Whizzy with a swipe of his razor sharp claws.

My brother immediately shot back, zapping Goren out of the sky. Goren spun uncontrollably before crashing. Then Whizzy turned his anger on the vortex produced by Javid as it was bearing down on him.

Whizzy knelt down to brace himself before unleashing a bolt of lightning. It hit the tornado, which lit up from inside. The winds immediately slowed and the whirlwinds disappeared, revealing the injured sorcerer. Javid spun on the ground a few more time before sliding to a stop curled in agony.

The bolt had struck him in the leg. A large wound was easy to see. Javid writhed in pain, grunting and screaming.

Whizzy kept his wand fixed on its target. I joined him, as did Grandpa. Even Grace held an arrow to her brother...and I was certain she would fire first.

"It's over, Javid," Grace announced. "You have lost."

The injured elf continued to roll around in agony. "Master! Master!" He yelled like a lunatic.

"Shut up, you crazy..." Whizzy began to bark but our grandpa stopped him.

"Let him. Maybe he will summon the sorcerer we need," Grandpa explained.

It happened so quickly that I am still not sure how he arrived, but Sorcerer Pierre LaCroiux was suddenly standing before us. He wasted little time speaking. The wicked henchmen of Cragon Cadieux went directly after Grandpa...the strongest of us.

I just saw my grandpa's shadow fly across the nighttime skyline before hitting Kiefer's body with a loud thump. The impact knocked his wand clear from his paw. Grandpa landed on his stomach then rolled over on his back.

Whizzy didn't stand a chance either. He had turned to watch our grandpa's flight, courtesy of LaCroiux, when he too was tossed through the air.

I sprinted to Grace and pulled her behind Kiefer for cover. LaCroiux simply

lifted the giant butterfly from the ground
with the wave of his hand and sneered at us
as we cowered behind our friend.

He had become so powerful...and
vengeful. I could sense his hatred. It was in
his eyes how much he despised us all. A deep
red flame burned in his eyes.

He pulled roots from the ground to
tie my hands and feet. He did the same to
Grace and Phillip. Phillip was still woozy
from his earlier battle with Javid's vortex.

Sorcerer LaCroiux vanished and then
instantly reappeared above me.

I screamed.

"Oh...my poor dear, do you fear me?"
the evil sorcerer chuckled as he tormented
me. He held out his hand and moved it
directly over my face without touching me. I
could feel the heat from his palms...the
energy within him waiting to come out. It
was frightening.

"LaCroiux, you must face me!" Grandpa Whizzenmog proclaimed.

He and my brother remained free.

I had never been so afraid in all my life when a smile overcame that wretched, evil elf's face.

LaCroiux slowly turned and challenged my grandpa. I could still feel the chill in my body from the smile on his face even after he had turned. It was too sinister to explain.

"I believe you are right, Rainer," LaCroiux calmly replied before turning over his right hand and casting a spell on Whizzy.

My brother's fox face contorted in pain. His body became limp, and he crumpled to the ground. Then roots exploded from the ground and wrapped around his ankles, wrists and neck.

"Let's see if you can defeat me before your grandson runs...out...of...air," LaCroiux challenged.

Grandpa wasted no time lashing out.

SHRUBBERY BOMBS

23

Flashes erupted followed by thunderous claps as a powerful wizard battled against a dangerous sorcerer. They attacked with ferocious strength as their bodies blurred in motion.

Grandpa Whizzenmog's eyes glowed in the darkness. The gray fox sprang into the air, flipped over Pierre LaCroiux, fired a spell and landed gracefully on the other side.

The sorcerer blocked the wizard's attack with a swat from his bony hand, and pivoted on his leg to face Grandpa as he landed. LaCroiux turned both hands palm up and pulled upward as if he was holding something heavy.

The ground beneath Grandpa lifted sending the wizard tumbling backward. He caught himself before falling. Grandpa dropped to one knee and flicked his wand like he was cracking a whip. Then he yanked back causing Sorcerer LaCroiux's legs to come out from underneath him.

The crafty old elf summoned a gust of wind to catch him. LaCroiux dangled in the air a few feet above the ground.

Grandpa Whizzenmog took the opportunity to zap the roots holding Whizzy. They crumbled and fell from his neck allowing Whizzy to breathe again.

LaCroiux got back to his feet, but began to run away from Grandpa.

My grandpa furrowed his brow and yelled, "STOP!"

The evil sorcerer didn't respond. I struggled to break free from the thick, strong roots holding me hostage, but without my wand I was helpless.

Grandpa chased after LaCroiux, who had run a short distance and stopped.

"Where do you think you're going?" Grandpa Whizzenmog demanded.

The elderly sorcerer still refused to acknowledge Grandpa. He began to reach to the sky as though he was pulling on a rope.

"I have a surprise for you, Whizzenmog," LaCroiux mumbled.

A whistling noise grew.

"What is that sound?" Whizzy called out to me.

The high pitch sound grew louder and closer. Then an explosion between Whizzy and me tossed fragments of grass, leaves, dirt and rocks all over us.

Grandpa whipped back around when the sound hit his ears. "Children?" He shouted.

New whistling sounds hung in the air followed by a series of explosions.

"Bombs!" Grandpa called out as he ran back to free us. His battle with LaCroiux would have to wait.

The gray fox nimbly dodged the exploding shrubbery. I watched in amazement. Grandpa Whizzenmog dashed from side to side avoiding the bomb's impacts. A circular shrubbery bomb headed for a collision course with the fleet-footed fox. Grandpa noticed it at the last moment and slid underneath the fast moving bomb. It detonated only a few feet behind Grandpa.

When he reached me, I was free within seconds. He moved quickly and freed us all.

Sorcerer LaCroiux continued to create havoc summoning his shrubbery bombs. They scattered throughout the battlefield.

One slammed into the face of a nearby spider. It splattered leaves across the spider's eyes, blinding it. The hairy arachnid stumbled and collapsed, causing its Grimmiad rider to topple over and fall to the ground.

"We have to stop, LaCroiux!" Phillip shouted.

"Ya think?" Whizzy crassly responded. He was breathing heavily and rubbing his neck. "This guy is really starting to bother me."

"We will have to do this together," Grandpa commanded. "He has become too powerful to defeat on my own."

Sorcerer LaCroiux continued to assault the Grimmiads with his magical shrubbery bombs, exploding throughout the grasslands.

The vampire bats had returned and swarmed directly above us. Goren screeched loudly and dove directly at me.

I panicked. My heart was racing. I froze. At the last second, Phillip jumped and knocked me out of the way as Goren swooped past swiping his razor sharp claws at me.

I landed hard on the dirt. When I rolled over, Goren was nowhere in sight, but many other vampire bats were. Dozens circled over us in the night sky, like airplanes waiting to land at a busy airport.

"Where's, Goren," I yelled while searching the skies above.

"There!" Phillip croaked as he pointed.

Goren had reappeared; he was perched atop a nearby wolverine soldier's shoulders. He hissed at Whizzy and me. The bone thin vampire jumped down and began throwing rocks in our direction.

Whizzy quickly responded by firing a spell, freezing the grass blades next to him. He grabbed hold and snapped one of the grass blades. Whizzy spun around and swung the frozen blade, like a baseball bat, with all his might, hitting one stone right back at Goren.

The vampire bat ducked as the rock zoomed by this head, but it sliced his ear.

"AHHHHHRRRGGGG!" Goren yelled in pain and then jumped skyward disappearing from sight in the night sky.

The spell wore off and the blade of grass became limp in Whizzy's hands.

"That was pretty impressive," Grace Tallon complimented the reddish-orange wizard fox.

"You know it was," Whizzy brashly responded. A smile beamed across his furry face.

Grace scoffed at the fox's brazen reply.

I saw her smile when she walked away from my brother.

"Look out!" Phillip shouted.

A shrubbery bomb crashed down in the middle of us. It detonated with great force, throwing me, Whizzy and Grace.

I landed on my back. The stars in the sky above me blurred on impact. Everything was out of focus, like being cross-eyed.

I could hear Whizzy call out in pain.

I tried to get to my feet but couldn't. I had hit my head when I landed. A green fuzzy blob grew larger in front of me.

"Stop!" I shouted, placing my hand out in front of me.

A green hand grabbed hold of mine. It was Phillip's. I could tell because it was damp and clammy.

"Rachel, it's me, Phillip." He rubbed the back of my hand with his.

I closed my eyes and inhaled deeply.

Phillip pulled me close to his chest and wrapped his arms around me tightly. I could feel his heart pounding against my cheek.

"It's gonna be ok, Rachel," he spoke in a semi-reassuring tone. I could tell he was trying to convince himself too. "I found something that belongs to you." He held out his webbed hand.

Even with my eyes closed I knew immediately that it was my wand.

Before I could say thank you, another explosion erupted behind me. My eyes opened. I could see clearly again.

"Whizzy! Behind you!" I screamed to my brother as a large wolverine soldier raised its sword above its hairy head.

My brother rolled to avoid being sliced in half as the metal blade sparked against a stone in the dirt when it slammed into the ground. Whizzy had barely escaped. He scrambled backward on his backside to get away.

Meanwhile, Grandpa and LaCroiux had started their quarrel again.

The sorcerer twisted his white braided beard around his finger as a sinister smirk crept across his dirty face.

"Come on, sorcerer. Make your move!" Grandpa Whizzenmog challenged. He stood prepared for the sorcerer's attack.

Pierre LaCroiux reached down and tore two blades of the tall dark green grass from the ground. He began swinging them around like massive swords.

Grandpa backed away from the sorcerer's attack.

"It's time to see what you're made of, Whizzenmog!" LaCroiux laughed as he swung at the gray fox. "Hold still...and I promise this will be over quickly, Rainer!"

"We have to help them!" I pleaded with Phillip. My brother and my grandpa both needed our help.

"I'll help Whizzy," Phillip said as he pulled a Grimmiad sword from its sheath at his hip.

I ran to help my grandpa when I felt the hairs on my neck stand up. Something was following me. Just as I turned to see, a vampire bat grabbed me. It was Vella. I zapped her, causing us to crash. We tumbled along the ground. I landed on top of Vella, when she finally stopped.

My head was swimming. "I can't keep doing this," I cried. I tried to stand up, but fell back down. Everything on my golden foxy body hurt from my paws to my pointy ears. It was even painful to grip my wand, but that was the best protection I had so there was no way I was going to let go.

Vella didn't look any better. Blood trickled from her nostrils and mouth. She had a laceration across her cheek that bled onto the grass beneath us.

Phillip was faring better in his attempt to help my brother against the wolverine soldier. He was swinging away at the hairy beast from Wolverine Forest. The two enemies were trading swats...each ending with a clanging of metal.

Whizzy had gotten back up on his fox paws and pointed his crooked wooden wand at the wolverine, but couldn't get a clear shot as Phillip dodged a strike from the beast's sword.

"Get 'em, Whizzy!" Phillip yelped.

"Move outta the way!" Whizzy shouted back.

Grandpa continued to back pedal from the dangerous grass blades that Sorcerer LaCroiux spun above his head like a helicopter. The elderly sorcerer flung the blades at Grandpa, who leapt away just in time. The blades sliced into the ground and spun back into the air. They returned to their master like a boomerang. LaCroiux caught them easily and targeted his prey again.

I fired a spell to freeze the sorcerer, but he redirected the blast with his spinning blades. The bright blue bolt zapped a vampire bat, causing it to fall from the sky and crash into a wolverine and spider battling each other.

I kept firing, hoping something would hit him. It was at least keeping him from throwing that wicked grass blade back at my grandpa.

Grandpa Whizzenmog had regained his composure and aimed at the sorcerer once again.

"LaCroiux!" He barked, gaining the sorcerer's attention. Just then, Grandpa blasted a thunderous spell from his wand. It almost knocked him down.

Sorcerer LaCroiux deflected the blast. The force from its collision jarred the whirling blades free. The blades spun into the ground and fractured. LaCroiux was knocked down as the blast scorched across the battlefield.

It slammed into the wolverine battling Phillip and Whizzy. The beast groaned before falling to the ground with its eyes wide in pain. The massive creature fell forward and crashed down at the feet of Phillip.

"Did you do that?" Whizzy questioned his best friend.

"Ahh...no." Phillip shrugged and glanced at me.

I pointed to my grandpa with a smile on my face.

Our enemy was lying on the ground...wounded. His right arm was bleeding badly. He made awful noises as he attempted to get back to his feet.

"You were lucky, Rainer!" LaCroiux grunted in pain while holding his arm.

"And your luck has run out, LaCroiux." My grandpa raised his wand.

I did the same.

Whizzy and Phillip were walking toward us. My brother held his wand pointed directly at the nasty sorcerer.

LaCroiux's eyes jumped from wand to wand.

"He is trying to decide who to attack first," Phillip announced after reading the sorcerer's thoughts.

LaCroiux's face grimaced. He made a small movement toward the tall green frog.

Phillip grabbed his neck like he was being choked and fell to his knees, struggling for air.

Whizzy was enraged. He screamed without hesitation, "Signa." It was a spell that paralyzes the body.

I fired too, a freezing spell. "Ica!".

Grandpa fired at the same time I did, "Zeus!" A lightning bolt zipped from the tip of his wand.

I could see the spells racing toward Sorcerer LaCroiux. Three streams of magic were converging on the same target.

Whizzy's bright red spell hit first. LaCroiux's face turned rigid and pained. My bright blue freezing spell hit just a split second later turning the heinous elf's body a slight shade of blue. Grandpa's white-hot lightning bolt pierced LaCroiux's chest a moment later. The scorching bolt surged through the sorcerer's paralyzed and frozen body. His skin began to sizzle. Smoke rose from his head. A flash of white light brightened up the night. A zapping sound roared through the air like a fly got caught in an electric bug zapper.

Sorcerer LaCroiux was completely motionless...his hand still reaching out to choke our friend Phillip. His skin had changed to a dark gray color of a statue.

We gawked at Cragon Cadieux's henchmen. Suddenly, a gust of wind rushed across my back and slammed into LaCroiux. His body began to fall apart and fly away with the wind.

I gasped.

Sorcerer Pierre LaCroiux was gone.

WORDS OF WARNING

24

Grandpa Whizzenmog stood motionless. His face held a look of concern.

Whizzy excitedly pumped his fist in the air in celebration, "We did it!" He swung his fist like punching an enemy.

I couldn't speak. I didn't know how to react. We had just defeated Sorcerer LaCroiux...I should've been happy. Something immediately felt different in The Colossal Lands; there was a calmness.

"Is he dead?" Phillip asked as if he couldn't believe what he had just witnessed.

I was having the same feeling.

Goren swooped in and landed where the evil sorcerer had last been standing. He placed his razor sharp claws on the ground grabbing a claw full of dirt and dust.

"He has been returned to Mother Mistasia," the leader of the vampire bats explained. "You have freed us, Whizzenmogs." He spoke with a tone in his voice that sounded like gratitude.

The Wolverine Army had retreated. We found ourselves on a winning battlefield.

A cheer rose from behind. The Grimmiads began dancing around in celebration.

Phillip and Whizzy were doing some strange hi-five hand dance. They looked ridiculous. I couldn't help but smile at them. Phillip ran over and wrapped his thin amphibian arms around my waist and picked me up off the ground.

"We did it!" He yelled with a huge smile on his face.

My snout rubbed against his green cheek causing him to realize he was very close to me. Phillip set me back down and stepped back awkwardly.

"Sorry!" He apologized as he slightly blushed.

I could tell I was blushing too.

The gleeful frog ran away screaming excitedly, celebrating our apparent victory.

That was when I noticed Grandpa staring down at the spot where Sorcerer LaCroiux had been. While everyone else cheered like fools...he did not.

"Grandpa?" I called to him. I reached out and touched his forearm. "Is everything okay?"

He gave me a halfhearted smile and wiped away a tear from his furry cheek.

"Yes, my dear," he replied. My grandpa smiled and then he hugged me tightly.

The party continued on through the night. There was a joy in Mistasia that I hadn't seen since we last defeated Cragon Cadieux.

Grace Tallon was the only one that didn't celebrate. She walked to her brother's side, as Javid remained sitting injured in the grass. He was too weak to use his sorcery to escape.

The two were arguing, but I was too far to hear them. I suddenly wished that I had Phillip's powers of telepathy so I could eavesdrop on their conversation.

As I approached, it became clear that Grace was challenging her brother to rethink his choice of supporting King Cragon Cadieux, the last remaining sorcerer... besides her brother.

"How could you think fighting for him would make you stronger?" Grace scolded Javid. Her tone was cutting and abrasive.

"I have discovered things that few elves have ever learned. LaCroiux taught me the ways of a sorcerer...something you will never understand," Javid blasted back.

"No! I can't understand, and I don't want to, Javid! Our family fights to protect Cadieux Castle not rule it!" Grace replied.

"Rule?" Javid scoffed. "I don't want to rule, sister. I want to survive," the injured Elven sorcerer revealed.

Grace hesitated. She was trying to grasp what her brother could possibly mean.

Javid continued to explain, "King Cragon will rule Mistasia. I've chosen to follow him in order to survive. Anyone against him will be captured or destroyed, Grace," Javid appeared to be pleading his case in an attempt to convince his sister to join his side of this battle.

"No! How could you turn your back on those we are supposed to protect? We fight for this reason...to keep rulers like King Cragon Cadieux out of power." Grace gripped her sword handle at her side.

"How is that working out for you?" Javid crassly asked, since Cragon Cadieux was currently the king.

"Merran Cadieux is the rightful ruler of Mistasia, Javid. She will be once again," Grace defiantly boasted.

"I believe that you are fighting a losing battle. There is no defeating him," Javid's voice changed. He was scared.

"Look around, brother. Does this look like we are losing?" Grace pointed to the jubilant group of Grimmiads celebrating in the grasslands behind her. "Your powerful teacher is gone. How do you think King Cragon will react now?"

Javid simply replied, "You will find out soon enough."

TO CATCH A KING

25

The celebration in The Colossal Lands of Mistasia after the defeat of the terrible Sorcerer Pierre LaCroiux felt like they would have lasted all night, but one frightening moment brought it all to an end.

Grace had rejoined Phillip, Whizzy and me. Grandpa was again examining the dusty remains of LaCroiux like he was waiting for the elder sorcerer to instantly return before our eyes in a flash of light.

The vampire bats had gathered together, as did the giant spiders of The Colossal Lands with their dwarf-sized Grimmiad riders.

"Is this going to be a problem?" Whizzy wondered referring to the two groups huddling about on opposite sides of the grasslands as if waiting for the perfect time to strike.

"I don't think they like each other," I replied.

The wind rustled the once tall grass that had been crushed and trampled during the recent battle. Heavy gusts lifted the blades up off the ground.

A trembling began at my feet.

"What's happening?" Phillip asked with his large red eyes searching for an answer in the night sky.

"King Cragon?" Whizzy asked, gripping his wand against his chest to keep the wind from ripping it from his paw.

The ground near Grandpa Whizzenmog began to spin.

"A portal," the gray fox shouted over the winds. "Get back!" He motioned for us all to move away as he ran toward us.

The thunderous roar of the winds
seemed to cancel out all other noise. It hurt
my sensitive fox ears. Placing my paws over
them, I attempted to block the rushing
wind.

A shadowy figure appeared in the
portal.

The wind suddenly stopped and all
noise disappeared. It was eerily silent. A
pressure entered my ears. Nothing moved as
if someone had pressed 'pause'. Then a blast
of sound knocked everyone to the ground.
The portal had disappeared.

"Whizzenmog!" A deep growling voice
called into the night. The once shadowy
figure gained its shape directly before our
eyes.

"Cragon!" I gasped. The king had
ventured from his castle. He must have
really wanted the emerald badly to risk
coming here alone. He appeared tall and
strong. His beard was beginning to show

some aging as tiny gray hairs showed like imperfections on his well-groomed face.

Within an instant, vampire bats swarmed the king. He knelt and braced himself against the rushing winds from their wings.

The vampire bats continued to assault him. Loud ear piercing screeches erupted into the air.

I covered my ears. Whizzy did too. That was when I noticed that Grace and Phillip both held their swords at the ready. I could see Phillip's chest pounding as his heart raced. Mine was too. I didn't know what was worse...the booming from my heart or the high pitch noise echoing in my ears from the vampire bats.

King Cragon held his hands over his ears. He was wincing in pain.

Grandpa now stood beside me. He was covering his ears as well. His eyes never broke contact with the monstrous leader of

Mistasia. I could tell he was waiting for the opportune moment to strike.

The vampire bats had afforded us the chance to prepare while the evil king was wounded.

The slick gray fox released his grip on his large ears and readied his wand. With the flick of his wrist, Grandpa sent a wide bright green flash across the ground. It spread out underneath his target.

The hundreds of blades of grass stood up off the ground and marched toward the king as he struggled against the painful noise. He lashed out, knocking a single vampire bat out of formation, sending it crashing to the ground behind Whizzy and me. The green blades of grass, which now were half their original height, began wrapping themselves around Cragon Cadieux's limbs. First they attacked his arms and legs, and then encased his body until the defiant ruler was tightly held.

Grandpa fought to hold King Cragon captive.

"Grimmiads, now!" My grandpa shouted.

Three giant spiders rumbled toward the struggling king.

"Fire!" Gelna Grimmiad commanded. The three ugly, hairy black spiders began spitting webs.

The vampire bats narrowly escaped being captured themselves as the thick, wet, silken webs launched through the air and landed on the king, rendering him motionless.

GRANDPA'S SECRET

26

My grandpa's eyes were bloodshot and wet. He gritted his teeth so hard I could hear them cracking. I had never seen him so upset.

"Cragon!" Grandpa shouted as he hastily approached the restrained king.

The dark-haired, bearded elf had always resembled a human more than any other creature in Mistasia. His eyes were burning with aggression. A vein began to protrude from his forehead, as his face grew red from distress. Cragon Cadieux continued his attempt to free himself.

"Give me the emerald, Whizzenmog!" The pompous king demanded.

The gray fox zapped him.

I called out, "No!" I was shocked.
"Grandpa, don't!" I pleaded with him to
stop.

Whizzy grabbed our grandpa from
behind, stopping the gray fox from
continuing to torture the defenseless king.

"Grandpa, please. He can't harm us
now!" I continued to plead with him.

Everyone was still on edge, despite
King Cragon's current predicament. Phillip
and Grace continued to hold their swords in
defense. Whizzy and Grandpa held their
wands pointed at their enemy. Even the
Grimmiads and Vampire bats seemed
restless and uncomfortable.

I, however, felt at ease for the first
time since we arrived. All three sorcerers
were accounted for and currently subdued.
LaCroiux was dead, Javid was badly injured,
and now Cragon Cadieux was captured.

"Give it to me, you cowardly fox. It
belongs to me," Cragon shouted.

A strange silence fell over everyone. We had all heard him, but awaited my grandpa's response.

"It never belonged to you, Cragon!" Grandpa lashed back.

"The emerald belongs to my family, and you stole it!" The captive king revealed.

Grandpa zapped him again. Cragon yelled in pain. I stepped in, but the spell hit my arm.

I fell to the ground in pain.

"Rachel," Phillip shouted. He reached down and grabbed me.

I could feel a burning heat surging through my body like I was on fire inside. My legs and arms trembled. This was not normal magic...it was a dark, sinister magic!

"Grandpa!" Whizzy shouted.

"Control your emotions, Whizzenmog!" Grace scolded the elder fox.

Grandpa's eyes suddenly changed. His normal appearance returned, like a demon had left his body.

"Rachel, my dear, I am so sorry." Grandpa fell to his knees at my side and placed his hand on my face. He closed his eyes and began mumbling something.

The burning sensation quickly disappeared. A cool feeling took over like a blast of winter air rolled across my body.

When he opened his eyes, he must have seen the fear in mine.

"What did he mean, grandpa?" I asked. "Did you steal the emerald?"

Grandpa Whizzenmog didn't answer. The anger reappeared. He snapped to his feet and once again held his wand at the king. Its white-hot tip was glowing in the darkness.

"I was protecting the Cadieux family...something you wouldn't understand,

Cragon!" The sheer rage in my grandpa's voice was frightening.

"Protect?" King Cragon continued to challenge the gray fox. "Then you are a worldly failure, Whizzenmog!"

Grandpa's wand tip brightened.

"No!" I cried.

For an instant, Grandpa peeked over his shoulder at me. His wand dimmed again but remained lit.

"You couldn't do it then, and you won't now, Whizzenmog," the sorcerer sneered as his bright white teeth glowed amidst his thick black beard. "It's time you come clean, wizard. Tell your grandchildren of the hero you are. Tell them about your greatest triumph."

"No," my grandpa whispered as tears formed in his eyes. He lowered his wand, which was now pointed at the ground. Grandpa lowered his head as well, but said nothing.

"Remember, Whizzenmog. I certainly do. It was one of the greatest nights of my life," Cragon Cadieux continued to pressure the gray wizard fox into spilling the story. "It was the night I first became the King of Mistasia."

"Enough, Cragon!" Grandpa shouted. He raised his wand once again.

"You can tell us, Grandpa," Whizzy said in a reassuring voice. Then my brother looked to me to see if I agreed.

I nodded, hoping what we would hear next wouldn't be as horrible as it seemed.

"Not able to recall your greatest moment as the protector of the king and queen of Mistasia, Whizzenmog? Then let me refresh your memory. After all it has been many years since you ran away." Cragon smiled again.

Grandpa just glared at the evil king. He appeared ready to allow Cragon Cadieux to unlock whatever secret Grandpa

Whizzenmog held so tightly for all these years.

Suddenly, Grandpa broke his silence and interrupted the captured king before he could reveal the story.

"I knew I couldn't trust you, Cragon. Your brother knew too. Steven Cadieux was truly a great ruler and king...something you will never accomplish. But I never believed that you could corrupt so many minds." Grandpa paused as King Cragon grinned widely, showing pride in his devilry. "When I positioned Ethan to guard the Cadieuxs that night...I never thought. I never imagined the betrayal...from my own brother."

"It was pure genius to use Ethan Whizzenmog," Cragon began laughing.

"My own brother," Grandpa's rage erupted again. "AHHHH!" He screamed as he zapped his prisoner again.

King Cragon yelled in agony and fell to the ground, but resumed his laughter when the spell subsided. The Cadieux crown fell from the head of the king and rolled to his side. It shimmered slightly with the moonlight.

I placed my paws over my mouth and began to cry. Phillip hugged me.

"It was easily accomplished," Cragon chuckled as Goren pulled him off the ground.

"What?" Grandpa asked. "What was easily accomplished?"

"I know what you want to ask me, Whizzenmog. How did I corrupt your darling brother?" Cragon leaned forward slightly and whispered, "It...was...easy!"

"You are the most evil being I have ever met," Grandpa said.

"Why? Because I had my own brother killed so I could claim the throne! You would do the same." Cragon explained.

"No. No, I would never," Grandpa replied defiantly.

"Your brother did," Cragon responded.

"My brother was a fool to trust in you, Cragon. You are a deceitful and treacherous snake!" Grandpa Whizzenmog emotionally shouted.

"A snake." Cragon's face beamed with glee. "That reminds me of your brother, Whizzenmog. Do you know how he died?" The sinister king goaded the wizard fox into asking.

"No. How did he die?" Grandpa questioned.

A sinking feeling entered my stomach. I caught eyes with Phillip. I could see the fear in his red eyes.

"At the hands of your grandchildren's friend...the frog," Cragon revealed to the unsuspected gray fox.

Grandpa had been in Greenville then. That was when Ethan Whizzenmog appeared as a snake in our home. He captured and dragged me here. It was the first time Phillip, Whizzy and I came to Mistasia. He was Sorcerer LaCroiux's original apprentice. We had battled him in Cadieux Castle. Phillip eventually killed the corrupted Whizzenmog with Grace's sword.

"Phillip was protecting me, Grandpa," I explained.

Grandpa unexpectedly smiled. "For decades I have lived with the regret of those days. I never knew how deep your wickedness went Cragon. I just knew that when the king and queen were killed, you had everything to do with it! So I removed the last emerald from Cadieux Castle, opened a portal to leave Mistasia, and hoped that someday I could return to see your demise," the wizard fox declared. "My grandchildren have come to Mistasia to turn that wish into a reality. They will end your rule over these creatures, Cragon Cadieux. Your time is coming to an end."

MIND IMAGES

27

Grandpa Whizzenmog conjured up a spell that encased Cragon Cadieux, the current King of Mistasia, in a magical bubble to hold him securely.

The sun had begun to rise in The Colossal Lands. That meant we were another day closer to returning home before our parents could discover we had disappeared.

I felt at ease. We were all together– Phillip, Whizzy, Grandpa and I. We were all uninjured, and we had finally captured the king. All that remained was to find Princess Merran Cadieux, free her from the sorcerer's magic and once again aid her in becoming Queen of Mistasia.

Vampire bats now stood watch over Cragon Cadieux. The captive king was eerily calm like he was meditating.

Whizzy slept on a makeshift bed of grass. Grace stood guard over her brother, Javid. The injured Elven sorcerer hadn't moved in hours, but Grace was making certain he didn't try to escape. Grandpa hovered around Cragon Cadieux, keeping a close eye on the powerful sorcerer king. Phillip and I sat together next to Whizzy.

"Thank you, Phillip," I said.

"For what?" He replied with an uncomfortable giggle.

"Just for being here with me. I know that I didn't always treat you very well in the past...I'm sorry," I had truly been awful to Phillip Harper for years. He was always my brother's annoying best friend. That was until last summer. It is amazing how differently you can see someone that you have known for years after just one experience with them. I never even considered that I could have feelings for him, but now I do.

Phillip played with some dirt with his left hand, while avoiding eye contact. "Don't worry about it. That's okay." He replied.

"No, Phillip...it isn't." I placed my paw on his cheek and turned his head to face me. I looked into his big red eyes and smiled. My heart fluttered, then he surprised me with a kiss. It was quick and wet...he is a frog. I was just happy he didn't use his tongue.

Phillip quickly looked down again, but I placed my paw on his cheek again. He turned his head on his own this time and we kissed again.

"Hey! Stop that! Gross, Phillip," Whizzy shouted. He pelted us with chunks of grass. "I don't wanna see that ever again."

"Whizzy?" I started to argue, but he just pointed his wand at me.

"I'll zap you!" He joked.

The three of us sat in uncomfortable silence on the ground with Phillip in the middle. Out of the corner of my eye I saw my brother hold up his paw. Phillip punched it in celebration, like boys do when they do something cool. A smile came over me. My brother had finally realized that if anyone was going to date his sister...it should be his best friend. At least I wasn't dating Billy Lawton.

It had been almost six hours since my grandpa and King Cragon had verbally battled. In that time we had watched the sun rise and Phillip had kissed me, two things that I would have normally enjoyed, but by now I was becoming fidgety.

"We need to return to the castle," Grace said, startling Phillip and me. Whizzy just turned around and waved like an idiot.

"Hi, Grace," he said.

"Your grandpa sleeps, when we need to be moving to free the queen," Grace demanded.

I hadn't realized that our grandpa was sleeping.

"He isn't sleeping. He's standing up, Grace!" Whizzy pointed to Grandpa Whizzenmog, who stood up facing King Cragon like a watchdog...or watchfox.

"I think he is sleeping, Whizzy," Phillip added backing Grace. "I can't reach him. I tried to speak to him, but there is no answer."

"He isn't a phone, Phillip. There won't be a voice message. Maybe he just doesn't want to talk to you," Whizzy snarled.

"Okay, but it's different in the mind of someone who is asleep. It is like a jumbled mess of words and sounds. Images swirl around like being in a toilet after you flush," Phillip graphically explained.

"Oh, nice, Phillip. That is disgusting!"
I suddenly got a vivid picture of a flushing
toilet.

"Like right now I can see images in
your mind, Rachel."

"Really? What do you see?" I eagerly
asked.

Phillip paused for a moment,
"Ahhh...maybe I'll just do Whizzy's mind,"
Phillip said bashfully.

"No, I don't ever want to know what
is going on in this Whizzenmog's mind,"
Grace said before urging Phillip to answer
my question.

"Err...I can see us kissing. I feel
warmth and happiness," Phillip replied as he
blushed.

I suddenly couldn't stop smiling.

"Phillip, that's your mind, you twit.
Try someone else," Whizzy demanded.

"Oh, this is ridiculous. I'll just go over
there." I got up and walked over to my

grandpa. He stood perfectly still. His chest moved in sequence with his breathing. He was very peaceful.

I didn't speak for fear that he would awaken. When I saw his face, I noticed that his eyes were wide open but glazed over. He didn't blink. It was like no one was there. I waved my paw in front of his face and had no reaction, like he couldn't see me.

I shrugged my shoulders in reply back to my brother. Grandpa definitely appeared to be sleeping. When I started to walk away, a flash of green light caught my eye. On my grandpa's wrist was the green emerald bracelet. I peeked at his face to see if he was watching, but he continued to stare at King Cragon. I placed my paw over the emerald bracelet. Warmth flowed through my paw and up my arm. It pulsed into my ear. I pulled my arm back and again looked at grandpa. He didn't react. The power surging from the emerald was tremendous. It was drawing me to it like the emerald was calling me to take it. Again I reached for the bracelet. When I touched it, a spark shot from its center. I fell to the ground.

My grandpa awoke violently, stumbling to his knees. He shook his head. The green bracelet went completely black and fell from his wrist into the grass.

"Rachel?" Grandpa looked at me with confusion in his now normal eyes.

A feeling of panic came over me.

He realized something was wrong immediately after looking at me. "What is it, my dear?" Then, he noticed the bracelet was gone. "NO!" He shouted. "Where is it?"

The magical prison holding the devilish King Cragon had vanished. In an instant the calm atmosphere of The Colossal Lands turned into a terrifying horror.

The evil sorcerer king had been waiting for the moment he could break free, and this was it. He tore through the spider webs holding him in seconds.

Grandpa jumped in front of me as the king punched the ground sending a tidal wave of debris in our direction.

I didn't have time to react. I wouldn't have even known what to do, but grandpa raised both arms, forming a wall with the grass blades that were on the ground around us. The debris slammed into it like a monstrous wave from an ocean. Its power was tremendous, but Grandpa's wall held long enough to save us both. Grandpa was knocked down from the impact, landing next to me.

King Cragon Cadieux reached to the ground and picked up his crown, placing it on his head. Next, he summoned a tiny funnel of wind that danced around beside my grandpa and me. It sucked the bracelet up and brought it to King Cragon.

Grace Tallon shot arrows at the unsuspecting king. The first sliced across his chest tearing his robes but only scratching his skin. He easily deflected the other into the ground. He raised his fist. When King Cragon opened his hand, a gust of wind knocked Grace to the ground. He held the bracelet in his hand as it morphed back into the shiny green emerald. He smirked at Grandpa Whizzenmog and then vanished with a loud clap of thunder.

King Cragon Cadieux had escaped with the last emerald.

MAKE THE RIGHT CHOICE

28

Chaos reigned in The Colossal Lands. The Grimmiads were loudly chanting, vampire bats swirled in the skies above us, Grace and Grandpa began arguing, and to top it all off King Cragon must have conjured up a terrific storm as the winds picked up and began whipping around us. Within seconds the clear sunny morning Mistasian sky changed violently. It was now dark and frightening. Flashes of lightning leapt from the clouds racing in all around us. They were on a collision course directly over us. Then the rains began, which was nothing like I had ever seen in Greenville. Drops of rain exploded on the ground. They hit with such force it hurt.

"Kiefer!" I yelled to our winged friend. The giant butterfly landed and opened his wings to protect us from the winds and rain.

"You know we have to destroy it!" Grace yelled at Grandpa resuming her argument.

"I won't do that elf!" He barked back in a disrespectful tone.

I had never heard my grandpa speak so rudely toward anyone before. It shocked me.

"If you don't Whizzenmog, then I will!" Grace gave an ultimatum. She gripped her sword handle at her side.

"Stop it!" I yelled.

"I don't take orders from an elf," Grandpa growled at Grace Tallon while ignoring my plea for them to stop arguing.

The two combatants were mere inches away from one another. Whizzy and

Phillip stepped in to pull them, but Grace and Grandpa continued to argue.

"Shut up!" I screamed over the winds and pouring rain.

Suddenly, everyone stopped.

"We need to get to Cadieux Castle. Save your anger for the enemy that deserves it." I was frustrated and fed up.

"She's right," Grandpa Whizzenmog conceded. He looked ashamed of his behavior. "Kiefer, can you get us there?" He asked of the large butterfly shielding us from the weather.

Before Kiefer could respond, Grace interrupted. "I think I have a better solution." She walked away briskly and pulled her sword from its sheath to point it at her brother, Javid. "You will open a portal to the castle!" She demanded.

Javid scoffed. "Not likely, my sister."

Grace pushed closer. The tip of her sword touched Javid's Elven skin at the neck.

"Your master left you here...all alone, brother. He abandoned you."

"He...but...he couldn't," Javid stammered to explain the king's actions.

"You mean nothing to him. You are just another servant. Disposable. Replaceable," Grace jabbed verbally. "Here is your opportunity to make this right, Javid. Brother...open the portal."

"But I don't have the strength," he answered.

"I believe you do. You always did, but you were just waiting for him to save you. You knew it would be too difficult to escape alone. You knew that he would come for the emerald, but you were mistaken in thinking you would leave with him." Grace continued to explain the errors of Javid's trust in the Sorcerer King of Mistasia.

Javid's bottom lip trembled with anger. He knew that Cragon Cadieux had abandoned him.

"You can do this, Javid. It is the right choice." Grace lowered her sword and stowed it back in its sheath. Then she held out her hand.

Javid just looked at the extended hand of his sister for a moment. He grabbed hold and pulled himself up. Grace half smiled, and whispered something to Javid. She took a few steps backward allowing her brother room to work. He squatted down and winced in pain. The Elven sorcerer closed his eyes and put his arms out straight in front of him. He moved his hands in a circular motion.

As the rains continued, Javid conjured a small portal. It looked weak and unstable. Javid was exhausted. "Hurry!" He shouted. "I can't keep it open for long!"

"I don't trust him, Grace!" Whizzy shouted.

"Then trust me," she replied before grabbing Whizzy and pulling him into the portal with her.

They disappeared instantly.

"Whizzy!" I shouted.

"Come on, Rachel!" Phillip yelled. He grabbed my paw and hopped in to the portal, dragging me with him.

The ride was quick but rough. Phillip and I were tossed out on the other side. We landed in a fluffy, cold and deep snow pile.

Grandpa landed just behind us, but on his feet. Only four vampire bats managed to pass through the portal before it collapsed and closed.

"He did it," Grandpa acknowledged with surprised.

It was cold again in Mistasia; we had returned from The Colossal Lands back into the wintry weather outside Cadieux Castle.

Snow was stuck in my fur, so was Whizzy's as I saw him and Grace walking toward the silhouetted image of the castle in the distance.

We had returned in the exact spot we had left a few days earlier during our first battle with Sorcerer LaCroiux when he banished us to The Colossal Lands. Now a blizzard, probably compliments of King Cragon, raged.

"We have little time," Grandpa called. "I need to get that emerald back!"

"We must destroy it, Rainer!" Grace emphatically demanded.

"I will not discuss it, elf!" The elder gray fox scowled as snow built up along his cheeks and eyes.

"Stop it," I pleaded again.

"Look," Phillip pointed to a green hue lighting a window atop Cadieux Castle.

"The emerald," Grandpa replied.

We lumbered through the snow as quickly as we could. It was becoming increasingly more difficult with each passing second as the snow grew deeper and deeper. As we reached the walls of the castle the drifts of snow reached nearly twelve feet high. It aided our entrance into the castle. We would be able to climb the snow and enter through windows along the second floor instead of using the main entrance where King Cragon would most certainly have guards awaiting our arrival.

Grace led the way to the room where we had seen the green light from outside. Grandpa followed close behind. Phillip and I stayed close together as Whizzy brought up the rear.

It wasn't long before we encountered the first of the King's minions sent to stop us.

A single troll blocked the hallway. His body was so large it consumed everything.

The dumb-looking creature's pear-shaped head rubbed along the ceiling.

Grace didn't even break stride as she pulled an arrow from her pack and launched it from her bow, piercing the troll's neck. The ugly monster roared. Grace leapt. She bounced from the stone wall higher into the air landing on the troll's shoulder.

"Phillip!" she yelled. Grace grabbed hold of the arrow stuck in the troll's neck and pulled hard.

The troll cried in pain and leaned back.

Phillip winked at me, then hopped into action. He bounded at the troll-webbed feet first. Phillip landed with all his strength against the troll's chest sending it toppling over and crashing to the ground.

We dashed past the falling creature. Grace performed a back flip from the falling enemy's shoulder and landed next to Grandpa. She resumed the lead and directed us through the stone hallways of Cadieux Castle toward King Cragon.

We passed an unlit hallway when a low rumble began behind us.

"We have company!" Whizzy shouted.

"Wolverines!" I added after turning around.

There were four wolverines chasing us.

"I've got them," Whizzy called. "Keep going!" He shouted to Grace.

I skidded to a stop to help my brother. Phillip did too.

"Rachel?" Phillip started to ask.

"Keep going...I'm gonna help Whizzy." I held my wand directly at the lead wolverine as it closed in on us.

"Whizzy, duck!" I shouted. "Bombastic!" I called as my wand exploded in a bright yellow flame.

Whizzy leapt to the side as the spell closed in. It impacted the lead wolverine knocking it backwards, crashing into another.

The remaining two wolverines were very angry and ignored Whizzy as he lay on the floor in order to charge at me.

When they passed by, my brother stepped up and blasted them from behind with the same spell.

"Bombastic!" I heard his voice call out, followed by a bright yellow light.

I closed my eyes and slid to the wall to avoid the flying wolverines. The two beasts crashed to the floor in a heap.

They didn't look good when we ran past to rejoin our friends. Phillip was waiting for us just around the corner.

"They went up these stairs," Phillip said as he led the way.

Before us was a dark staircase. We slowly climbed when I lit the corridor with my wand. At the top was a heavy door. Phillip slowly pushed it open. Standing in

the middle of the room was our enemy,
King Cragon Cadieux, and he seemed to be
awaiting our arrival.

KING'S PROCLAMATION

29

The room was poorly lit and empty. There was nothing but stone floors and walls, except a single statue in its center.

"Princess Merran," I gasped.

"Let her go, Cragon!" Whizzy heroically barked.

The sorcerer king only smirked. He was calm and arrogant. It was obvious that he believed that he had won. He did possess the emerald, and held the future queen captive in the castle she was supposed to rule, but there were five of us and only one of him.

"Give up, Cragon. You don't stand a chance," Grace confidently demanded.

The king inhaled deeply. A plume of white smoke flowed from his mouth when he exhaled into the room. It hung in the air, floating toward the Elven protector to the princess. It began to change form and take shape right before us. The cloudy formation stretched and grew into long tentacles. It wrapped itself around Grace.

The three wizards, Grandpa, Whizzy and I immediately focused our wands at Cragon Cadieux.

"Release her!" Grandpa commanded.

"Whizzenmog, come now. You know that is not going to happen. She is my prisoner," Cragon replied.

Grace attempted to break free. Phillip helped by pulling on the white tentacles, but couldn't get a grip.

"Just like her," Cragon placed his hand on the stone figure in the center of the cold room.

He leaned closer and held out his left hand in which a flame emerged. Cragon blew at the flame causing it to touch the stone figure of Princess Merran's face. Suddenly, her appearance changed. Princess Merran's normal face appeared, though her body was still stone.

She gasped for air like she had been trapped underwater.

Grace Tallon finally freed herself from the king's sorcery. "Princess?" She called to her leader.

Grandpa started to move forward.

"Don't move!" Cragon demanded. "You stay right there," he said as he cast a devilish charm on us all.

The floor began to melt and cover our feet, trapping us in place.

"Uncle, what have you done?" the frightened princess questioned of her family member.

"Merran, I am just doing as I always have," he said in a sarcastic tone. "I'm doing what is best for Mistasia. Now, I want you to see this for yourself."

"See what?" she began to become upset.

"I want you to watch me destroy them." The evil king whispered into her ear. "With this." He held the last emerald in his hand.

The normally shiny green jewel looked dim and black in the sinister hands of the king.

Princess Merran composed herself. "You can't do that, Uncle. These are good creatures. They will do you no harm if you set me free," she attempted to reason with an unreasonable mind.

King Cragon had no intention of letting anyone in this room go. He couldn't if he wanted to remain ruler of Mistasia.

"I am the unquestionable ruler of Mistasia, and now with the Cadieux Emerald in my possession I am unstoppable," Cragon boasted. "You will remain my prisoner forever. Just like you planned to do to me," he reminded her. "How quickly you seem to forget that I was frozen in a dungeon...trapped in this castle for thirteen years, while my niece pretended that I didn't exist. You would have left me there to rot!" He spat his words at the statuesque princess.

"That is no trinket you hold, Cragon," Grandpa Whizzenmog reminded the king.

"Whizzy, you must destroy it," Grace whispered to the red-haired fox.

"Do you understand the consequences of destroying this jewel, fox?" King Cragon scolded. "You would lose your life."

I pointed my wand at the brooding king, "Don't threaten him again!"

"He isn't, Rachel," my grandpa replied. "The lore of the emerald states that anyone who destroys the gemstone will lose their life," Grandpa explained.

"Then I'll do it," Grace yelled as she drew back her bow and let an arrow fly.

King Cragon calmly snatched the arrow in his hand. "Your services are no longer needed in this castle, elf!" he replied. Cragon lifted his leg and then slammed his foot on the stone floor. The stones cracked and crumbled opening a gap in the floor, which Grace fell through and disappeared.

Our feet had been released when the stones began to crack. We were free. The four of us instantly attacked.

DEMISE OF A WIZARD

30

King Cragon Cadieux gripped the emerald tightly while defending himself. We attacked him from all four corners of the stone walled room. He seemed to anticipate each move, deflecting our attacks and using them against us.

Grandpa nearly took a blast from my wand in the face after the king redirected it with his hand. Whizzy fell to the ground when his own paralyzing spell was catapulted back at him. It hit his left leg. Phillip too barely dodged a rouge spell from Grandpa's wand. It singed the stone wall behind him.

I saw the gray figure of my grandpa running toward the king as he battled me. I tried everything I could imagine to keep him occupied, but the powerful king crushed each spell.

King Cragon punched the ground. The shaking caused me to tremble to my knees. I had only half stood up when I witnessed the tall black robed leader of Mistasia turn and hit my grandpa in the chest with his fist...the same one that held the emerald. A flash of green lit the room.

I screamed, "NO!"

My grandpa's face looked horrified. He cried out in agony and collapsed to the floor.

Cragon stood over him and raised his arm to finish him off.

Phillip leapt into action landing on King Cragon's back. The strong king's legs buckled slightly. Phillip jabbed his sword into the king's shoulder.

"Arrrg," King Cragon Cadieux cried in pain. He grabbed his wounded shoulder, when Phillip reached back again.

My grandpa suddenly sat up, wand in hand, and fired a spell at the emerald in King Cragon's right hand. The light from Grandpa's wand pierced the dim jewel, causing it to light up and shoot rays of green light shot across the room.

"No!" the wicked king bellowed.

Phillip swung his sword again cutting King Cragon's hand holding the emerald clean off.

The king fell to the ground in agony. Phillip began to fall too. King Cragon Cadieux reached out for the now glowing white emerald. The moment the king wrapped his fingers around the emerald, it exploded.

Phillip and grandpa where thrown in opposite directions. Each crashed into the stone walls. The light was so bright. It engulfed the entire room.

Then silence.

A female voice called my name. I could feel a soft hand rubbing my shoulder.

Grandpa! I thought and suddenly I was awake again.

Princess Merran Cadieux was kneeling before me. She looked distressed.

"Rachel, wake up!" she shook me vigorously.

Grace ran into the room. "Princess!" she called out with her sword drawn. "You are alive!" Grace happily replied after seeing Princess Merran still alive.

"Yes, Grace. I am alive," she replied solemnly.

The room was a disaster. Chunks of stone where scattered around the room.

My heart was beating so quickly. I was breathing heavily. Finally, I spotted my brother.

"Whizzy!" I shouted.

He was covered in a dusty powder from the crumbling stone scattered around him.

"Rachel," he coughed. "Where is Phillip?"

We instantly searched for the distinct green-colored skin of our frog friend.

"There he is!" I shouted with excitement.

Phillip was sprawled out in a far dark corner. He was amazingly uninjured.

"You are so lucky," I said as I hugged him tightly.

"Rachel," Whizzy called my name.

The sound in his voice told me everything I needed to know. He had just seen our grandpa...and it wasn't good.

When I turned around, Whizzy was on his knees uncovering our grandpa who lay underneath hundreds of fragments of stone.

Phillip and I joined him as we all frantically worked to free Grandpa Whizzenmog.

I gasped when Whizzy pulled away a chunk of stone to reveal our grandpa's face. It wasn't the gray fox that I expected. Underneath the dust and dirt was the aged human face of our true grandpa, Rainer Whizzenmog from Greenville. The one we had know all of our lives until the past few days in Mistasia.

"Is he alive?" Phillip gulped.

A began to cry as I covered my mouth with my paw. "He can't be dead."

"He has lost his life," Grace coldly remarked.

"Shut up!" Whizzy cried.

"No! He isn't dead," I yelled at Grace, hoping that would change everything.

"He has lost his life in Mistasia," Grace said again. "Your grandpa chose to sacrifice his life as the wizard fox. The image you see before you is no longer alive here in this world, but he has not died," Grace continued.

"I don't understand. Is he dead or alive?" my head was beginning to ache.

"Grandpa, wake up; it's Whizzy?" my brother said while crying.

I couldn't remember the last time I saw him cry.

"His life has ended here in Mistasia, Rachel. Your grandpa will be waiting for you in your world," Princess Merran reassured.

I couldn't begin to explain how happy I felt hearing that my grandpa would be waiting for us back home. I didn't know whether to cry or celebrate. I was so proud of my grandpa. He had shown such bravery. He sacrificed his life as Rainer the Wizard Fox to save us from the evil of Mistasia and in doing so destroyed the last emerald of power and the heinous Cragon Cadieux.

GRAND HALL TAPESTRIES

31

Queen Merran Cadieux once again was the ruler of Mistasia. My heart swelled with emotions to see her seated in the throne in the Grand Hall of Cadieux Castle. To know that we were the reason she sat there felt so rewarding.

Preparations for tonight's celebration were being made. A memorial for my grandpa was being created for tonight as well. Elves scurried about the castle hanging decorations, cleaning floors and preparing food as Phillip, Whizzy and I entered the Grand Hall.

It was a massive room with twenty-foot ceilings from which many large oval-shaped lanterns hung. The stone room was different from all the others in Cadieux Castle. It had a brightness, without any windows.

"Are these floors made of gold?" Phillip wondered. He looked at his webbed green froggy feet against the yellowish stone floor.

"They can't be," I laughed.

"This entire room is covered in gold," Grace's voice answered from behind us.

"That is friggin' awesome!" Whizzy so elegantly expressed.

Queen Merran and I caught eyes across the large room as she directed her Elven staff. She smiled at me.

I smiled too. It was so good to feel the calmness in Mistasia had returned. This world was so beautiful when the queen held the throne. Now that the sorcerers of Mistasia had been destroyed, maybe peace would remain.

"What are these?" I asked Grace pointing to dozens of long colorful decorative cloths hanging from the walls.

"Tapestries," Grace replied. "Each shows an important moment in our history."

"They are so beautiful," I said while looking at a picture of a red fox slaying a purple dragon. "Is that Whizzy?"

"That is your grandpa," Grace responded.

"He looks so much like, Whizzy?" I said with surprise. I had never imagined what grandpa would have looked like when he was a young fox protecting the king and queen before coming to Greenville.

"He was a lot like your brother then."

"Really? Like how?" I wondered.

"Angry and comical," Grace replied with a smile.

I started to ask Grace if she and my grandpa had been in love, but she must have

298

read my mind because she immediately stopped me.

"I was very close to Rainer. He was very important to me...to all of us here at the castle. That was why it was so hard when he left," Grace revealed. "We missed him dearly."

It was the most emotion I had seen Grace show...other than being angry at Whizzy.

"Who is that?" I asked after noticing another fox-like figure in the background of the same tapestry where grandpa battled the dragon. I pointed to the small golden fox casting a spell on another dragon.

"That is Ethan Whizzenmog," Grace sadly replied. "They were once so close...Rainer and Ethan. It destroyed your grandpa when his brother betrayed him. By the time you and Whizzy arrived in Mistasia, Ethan Whizzenmog was far removed from the striking fox he had been long ago."

During my conversation with Grace, Phillip and Whizzy had wandered around the Grand Hall looking at the other tapestries. Now they were across the room closest to the memorial that was being made for Grandpa Whizzenmog.

"Rachel! You've gotta see this!" My brother excitedly yelled.

I hurried across the golden room. Whizzy was pointing at a black tapestry behind him, and Phillip was hopping with excitement. They both had big smiles on their faces.

"What is it?" I asked.

"Look. It's us! All of us! We are all in this picture," Whizzy frantically tried to explain.

"Wow," was all I could say. The tapestry looked brand new.

"It was made in honor of your family's triumph," Queen Merran Cadieux proudly boasted.

"Cool," Phillip said.

"Awesome," Whizzy replied.

"It's beautiful. Thank you so much," I was amazed at how quickly it had been crafted.

The image was the battle we fought against King Cragon Cadieux. In it, Phillip was on Cragon's back holding a sword, while Grandpa shot a spell to destroy the emerald. Whizzy and I were also on the tapestry pointing our wands at the sorcerer.

"The entire Whizzenmog family of wizards, plus Phillip the Frog, will forever be honored in the Grand Hall of this castle," Queen Merran proudly spoke. "I am forever grateful for everything your family has done for mine."

Grace and the queen left to attend to the preparation for the celebration. Phillip, Whizzy and I now stood together. I reached out and held their hands. The memorial for Grandpa Whizzenmog was completed. A life size, colorful statue of the elder gray fox casting his final spell stood before us. He would continue to be at the queen's side in the Grand Hall forever.

ELVEN SURPRISE

32

Our return home was far different than the last. When we set out from Cadieux Castle the following morning the sun was shining brightly in the Mistasian sky. It was quite warm for a winter day with no clouds in the sky.

We were cheered from the moment we left the front of the castle until we reached the Whizzenmog house just beyond Wolverine Forest. Creatures of every kind we had ever encountered in Mistasia awaited our arrival. We saw Goren, Vella and Aevion, the vampire bats, Kiefer the Butterfly, and the Grimmiads. It was like we were in a parade.

Grace accompanied us. When we finally reached the spot we would return to Greenville, I felt sad.

"I will miss you, Grace," I said holding back tears.

"And I you, Rachel Whizzenmog." Grace hugged me. "You keep your brother out of trouble."

"Hey, I can keep myself out of trouble," Whizzy said sounding offended.

"I'm sure you can't, Michael Whizzenmog," Grace said jokingly to the red-haired fox. She leaned close and kissed Whizzy on the cheek. "Never forget me," she whispered into his ear.

Whizzy blushed as he smirked. "I won't."

Phillip pulled his sword from his sheath and extended the handle to the Elven warrior. "I guess I won't be needing this any longer."

"You can keep it," Grace replied.

"Ahhh...where would I keep a sword?"
He looked at Whizzy and me. "I don't think I
could begin to explain a sword to my
parents," Phillip joked as he handed it to
Grace. They hugged each other goodbye.

"How do we open the portal? The
emerald has been destroyed," Whizzy
bellowed.

"None of us know how," Phillip
added.

"We need a sorcerer," Grace
responded.

"What?" Phillip, Whizzy and I said in
unison.

"Each time you came to Mistasia in
the past...without your grandpa that is...you
were brought here by a sorcerer's hand.
Sorcerer LaCroiux to be exact." Grace
stopped speaking for a moment to turn
around.

Emerging from the Wolverine Forest was a small dark hooded figure. It walked toward us.

Whizzy pointed his wand at the small hooded figure.

Grace placed her hand on Whizzy's arm and lowered his wand. "This one is with me."

The figure stopped and pulled back its hood.

I gasped.

"Javid?" Phillip croaked. "I want my sword back, please!"

Grace hugged her brother. "Thank you for coming, brother."

We were all in shock. This couldn't be the same brother that had been helping Sorcerer LaCroiux because Grace seemed to be completely happy to see him.

"Grace, what's going on?" Whizzy asked. "Have you lost your mind?"

"No, Michael Whizzenmog. I have learned to forgive and forget...for the sake of my family. Seeing you and your sister together provides hope for us," Grace replied.

"So, are you ready to return?" Javid asked us.

Phillip and Whizzy didn't answer. Finally, I did. "Yes!"

"Have a safe trip," Javid smiled.

Suddenly, I had the urge to stay, but before I could change my answer the portal was stirring behind us.

Grace nodded to me and smiled.

I turned and leapt into the swirling portal and left Mistasia.

WHIZZENMOGS

33

I landed first. Phillip seconds later, and my brother bounced onto the snowy ground outside our sliding glass door in the backyard last.

It was a clear, sunny day in Greenville too. A soft wind blew against my human skin like a kiss. I exhaled. A puff of white hung in the cold air in front of my face.

We entered the house through the same door we had left from earlier this morning. It had been seven hours since we had left. Our parents wouldn't be home, yet from holiday shopping.

The house was eerily quiet.

"Grandpa," I called, but there was no answer.

Phillip and Whizzy followed me up the basement stairs. We had no idea where Grandpa Whizzenmog would be...we only hoped he was alive like Grace and the queen promised us he would be.

I went upstairs to the bedrooms. My heart was racing. I grabbed the handle to the room where he had slept. The door creaked. Whizzy was standing right behind me.

We walked into the room. In the bed something was definitely laying under the covers.

I grabbed hold and slowly pulled them back. I was terrified of what would be underneath them. I stopped when Grandpa Whizzenmog's face appeared. I gasped and then whipped the covers back completely.

"Is he here?" Phillip called from the hallway as he entered the bedroom.

Grandpa Whizzenmog appeared in the bed laying as he had in the castle after fighting Sorcerer Cadieux.

"Oh, no," Phillip cried as he covered his mouth. "I'm so sorry."

"Grandpa?" Whizzy placed his hand on Grandpa's shoulder. He stood on the opposite side of the bed.

I stared at my grandpa's face. He looked so peaceful...happy. I wiped away tears from my cheek with my sweatshirt.

"Rachel?" Whizzy looked at me confused. He was upset. "but Grace said..." He couldn't finish his sentence.

I leaned close and kissed my grandpa's forehead. "I love you," I whispered.

Suddenly, Grandpa began to stir. His eyes fluttered. Grandpa Whizzenmog awoke and shot up in bed.

We all froze.

"What just happened?" Phillip screamed in a high-pitched voice.

Whizzy and I wrapped our arms around our grandpa.

"Kids, you are all right," He sounded relieved. He hugged Whizzy. Then, he hugged me so tightly I thought he would never let go. "Ahh, my dear, Rachel. It is so good to see you all safe." He had tears in his eyes when he pushed back.

"We are safe. Everyone is safe. You did it Grandpa," I excitedly cried.

"Oh, it was so cool. After you...ahh, well...I mean when you were gone," Whizzy stammered. "We were at the castle with Queen Merran and Grace. They have this awesome room with stuff hanging on the walls." Whizzy animatedly explained.

"Tapestries, Whizzy," I interjected.

Grandpa Whizzenmog eagerly listened to everything. He had the proudest smile on his face.

"Yeah, and they had pictures on them," Whizzy kept going.

311

"You were on them," I told Grandpa Whizzenmog.

"And we were too," Whizzy said.

Grandpa began to laugh, because Whizzy was so excited.

"Ahh, it was awesome." Whizzy hugged our grandpa again. "I'm so glad you're alive!" He shouted.

"Well, I am too, my boy," Grandpa chuckled.

Phillip laughed.

The mood of the room calmed. Grandpa Whizzenmog and I smiled at each other.

"I'm so proud of you, Grandpa."

"And I of you, my dear."

I pulled his wand out of my back pocket and handed it to him. He gave it a peculiar look.

"It's your wand?" I said thinking he didn't recognize it.

"Not any longer," he sadly replied.

"Will you miss, Mistasia?" I asked him, knowing he wouldn't be able to return after sacrificing his powers to stop King Cragon.

Grandpa stood up and pulled me close. He took a deep breath and kissed my forehead. Then, he waved Whizzy over and held us both before he said, "I believe I have everything I need right here."

EPILOGUE

My life has experienced many changes since we first went to Mistasia just six short months ago. I feel like I've grown up so much. I've entered high school, grown closer to my brother, Whizzy, learned a great deal about my family history, and most importantly, I discovered sometimes the best things in your life are right in front of you...even if he is your brother's best friend.

Whizzy and I are closer than we have ever been. Our experiences in Mistasia made us realize just how important we can be to one another. Together we can accomplish anything.

My grandfather is doing very well too. He doesn't really talk much about Mistasia, but I think he misses it. In the meantime, Grandpa is spending a lot more time at our house than he used to. It is really nice having him around. He even gave Whizzy his wand. Grandpa told him, "A Whizzenmog shouldn't cast spells with a crooked wand."

The morning after we returned, Phillip Harper asked me out. I couldn't believe it. He had changed more than any of us. Like I said, it is funny how the best things in life are right in front of you. I had known Phillip almost all my life, but never thought he would become my boyfriend. Whizzy seems to be handling it pretty well. At first, he tried to tell Phillip and me we could only see each other on Wednesdays and Thursdays...because he had shows to watch on television those nights so 'his best friend' would be free then. We're still working on the schedule.

So what is next for me? I guess high school, then college and someday a family. But will I ever get to go back to Mistasia again...only time will tell. Maybe someday in the future Grace Tallon will reappear as an eagle at the basement sliding glass door ready to take all of us on another amazing adventure through the Land of Mistasia. Until then...we will have to wait.

FIND OUT MORE ABOUT

THE LAND OF MISTASIA

@

www.LandOfMistasia.com

PHILLIP & WHIZZY SHORT STORIES

 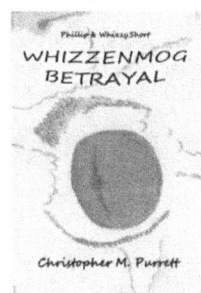

FIND OUT ABOUT OTHER STORIES FROM

CHRISTOPHER M. PURRETT

www.ChristopherMPurrett.com

ABOUT THE AUTHOR

CHRISTOPHER M. PURRETT

Christopher attended college at Central Michigan University, graduating with a degree in Broadcast & Cinematic Arts. There he met his wife,

 Misty, with whom he had two daughters, Lea & Kyra. The Phillip & Whizzy characters were born when he began telling bedtime stories to his daughters.

In his spare time, Christopher loves music, movies and sports, especially hockey and football. He lives in Michigan with his family.

Keep up with him at www.ChristopherMPurrett.com
Twitter
www.Twitter.com/CMPurrett
Facebook
www.Facebook.com/ChristopherMPurrett